CALL HER BLESSED

CALL HER BLESSED

Jeanette Gilge

Serenade/Saga
BOOKS
of the Zondervan Publishing House
Grand Rapids, Michigan

Heartfelt thanks to all the dear ones who prayed this book into existence and to Roy, Helen, Carl, and Olga for patiently answering countless questions.

J.G.

CALL HER BLESSED
Copyright © 1984 by The Zondervan Corporation,
1415 Lake Drive, S.E.,
Grand Rapids, Michigan 49506

ISBN 0-310-46452-8

Edited by Anne Severance and Nancye Willis
Designed by Kim Koning

Printed in the United States of America

85 86 87 88 89 / 8 7 6 5 4 3

To Emma Henrietta Meier
my grandmother
and
all women who rear children
not born to them

THE VERLAGER FAMILY TREE
(Emma and Al)

Children	Spouse	Grandchildren
Albert	Mamie	Paul, Arthur, Ruby
Fred	Helen	Kermit, Everett
Ellen (Ella)	Henry	Carl, Edward, Harvey, Harold, Myrtle, Grace, Jim
George	Sadie	Dorothy, Norma, Glen, Ardis, Owen, Betty, George, Jr., Bunetta, Gardia
Leonard	Nora	Elaine, Goldie, Shirley Emma, Joy Ann, Len, Jr.
Minnie	Nels	Amy, George, Rose, John
Edward (Eddie)	Connie	Allison, Shirley, Maybelle, Marylou, Richard, Edward
	Peggy	Rosemary, Gordon, Kathleen, Frank, Ruth
John	Esther	Jean
Gertrude (Gertie)	Joe	Clyde, Earl, Don
Roy	Helen	Ronald, Marilyn
Emma (Emmie)	Ed	Jeanie
Carl	Olga	Albert
Henry (Hank, Henny, Lefty)		

CHAPTER 1

A TINY BABY WAS CRYING—CRYING. Emma pulled the comforter up over her chilly shoulder, her thoughts floating between layers of unconsciousness. *Why doesn't someone see about it?* she wondered.

She certainly never had allowed *her* babies to cry like that. So long ago—all those babies.

Poor little thing. Maybe I should get up and take care of it. No, twenty years of crying babies is enough! Now it is someone else's turn.

Exhaustion claimed her again, but the crying continued. *Poor baby! So close. I'd better see—*

Emma heaved her body out of bed. The moonlit room snapped into focus as she opened her eyes. Baby Jean. Emmie's baby. *Her* baby now. How could she have forgotten—even in sleep?

She scooped up the tiny bundle, stuck her feet into slippers, and padded toward the kitchen.

"There, there, *Liebchen*," she crooned. Sleepily, she lit the little kerosene burner and poured milk into a blue-and-white speckled saucepan. The baby screamed in her ear as she stuck a funnel into the narrow bottle neck and filled it with warm milk.

Wrong! So wrong! This baby should be warm and cozy at its young mother's breast.

A sob, always close these days, erupted as she thought of that lovely young lifeless body lying up on the hill near Al's.

When the baby's cries gave way to the sounds of contented sucking, Emma leaned her head against the high-backed rocker.

The clock struck three. Three more hours of sleep—if the baby slept. Tired. So tired.

She felt the baby slipping from her arms and jerked. She shook her head. *Have to stay awake!* That hazy dream—if only it had been someone else's baby. If only she were still keeping house for Roy and Carl and Hank, free to help with the milking and feeding the chickens and gardening and knitting and talking on the phone—and sleeping all night through.

"O Father," she whispered. "I don't understand how You could let Emmie die and leave this little one. How can I start all over again? I'll be seventy-two when she graduates from high school!"

She eased the baby into her bassinet and crept into bed. *I could cry for a week but I don't have time. So behind with work—can hardly see out of the lamps—must wash those lamp chimneys tomorrow and bake bread and scrub floors and get started on the garden. And the baby will cry and cry.*

Ready to cry herself, she remembered that Gertie was coming! She smiled, sighed, and slept.

When Emma heard Roy and Carl go out to do chores, she

again hauled herself out of bed. Thank goodness she hadn't had to call them since the baby came. But her youngest, Hank—Henny, she always called him—was just fourteen, and a hard boy to understand. She decided to dress first and then go up and wake him instead of tapping on the ceiling with the broom handle. Might wake the baby.

Too late. The baby's little arms were waving and she was starting to cry.

Emma hurried to the kitchen, lit the kerosene stove and built a wood fire while the milk heated.

"Wouldn't you know it!" she muttered as the kerosene flame flickered and went out. "Empty."

Must tell Roy to buy more kerosene when he goes to Ogema to get Gertie, she thought as she lifted the smelly can and filled the stove.

By the time she had it filled and lighted, the baby was screaming. No need to go up to wake Henny. She tapped three sharp taps on the ceiling and his heel gave three answering taps.

When she had filled the bottle she quickly put more wood on the fire and settled down in the rocker with the baby.

No Henny.

Screaming baby in one arm, broom in the other, she tapped three I-mean-business taps and he answered with two I'm-coming thumps.

Eye on the clock, she eased herself back in the rocker. As the baby's cries ceased, she realized tension inside her had already begun to tighten like a huge clock spring. And the day had barely begun!

Ten minutes. No Henny. Roy and Carl were none too patient with him at his best. Oh, if he'd only hurry! Why did he always have to drag behind?

Ear tuned for the creak of his bed, she waited as the baby burped and dozed. She better get him up now, she decided,

9

before the baby went back to sleep. She headed for the stairs.

Halfway through the dining room, she heard him coming, sighed, and sat down again. She'd try to be patient.

As he laced his boots, tousled hair falling over his eyes, she said, "Henny, it would help so much if you'd get up when you hear the boys get up."

"Don't hear 'em."

"Well, then, get up as soon as I call you or rap."

"Yeah, yeah."

"Hurry up and help the boys. After breakfast, you can stay with the baby while I feed the chickens."

"Aw, Ma! All she does is bawl and I don't know what to do with her."

"All right! All right! Just get going now!"

The baby's little hands flew up as the door slammed, and Emma's tension spring tightened another notch.

"O Father," she whispered. "Why? Please help him do what he should."

Baby asleep again, Emma hurried to the kitchen and set the big black frying pan on the stove, spooned lard into it, and reached for the kettle of boiled potatoes she always prepared the night before.

Empty! "I know I planned to boil them. How could I forget?" she muttered. Well, they'd just have to eat more bread and a few more fried eggs.

She ground coffee, wishing she had thought to do it while the baby was awake, filled the pot, and was setting the table when Carl came in with the milk.

"When's that kid gonna start gettin' up and helpin' us? You know he only milked one cow this morning?"

Emma felt the spring tighten another notch. "It's so hard . . . I don't want to wake the baby."

"That's all I hear around here! 'Don't wake the baby!' "

10

He slammed the door before she could answer.

She turned and reached into the bread box. "Oh, no!" she wailed, holding a stub of a loaf. Now she'd have to fry pancakes.

The boys were washed and at the table before the first panful was done.

Roy shook his fork at Hank. "You clean the barn this morning. Carl's going to be out in the field and I'm going to town to get Gertie."

"But I gotta feed chickens . . ."

Carl tilted his chair back and let out a hoot. "Big job!"

Roy scowled at both of them. "You clean the horse barn too! When I was fourteen. . . ."

Hank waved his hand. "Oh, I know, I know. You ran the whole place single-handed."

"Boys! Boys! That's enough. Oh, forgoodnessakes, there's the baby again, and I have to make more pancakes!"

Carl unwound his long legs, headed for the bedroom, and came back awkwardly patting the baby who sounded like she might stop crying.

Emma gave Roy the first pancakes.

Hank growled.

"Henny, you hold your horses. Roy's got to get going. Gert'll be waiting. And you, too," she told Buckley, the little white terrier who sat a discreet distance from the table quivering in anticipation of leftovers. "Roy, you sure the roads are all right?"

He nodded. "Talked to the mailman yesterday. He said the sinkholes are the worst since he's been on the route, but I'll be careful."

After the boys had eaten and left for the morning, she poured a cup of coffee, speared a cold pancake, and tossed the rest to Buckley.

Quiet. Blissful quiet. She wanted only to sip her coffee

11

and think over the past weeks—maybe even cry to relieve that ache in her throat. No time. She did take time to tell herself again, *Emmie is gone! And the baby is here. Day after day she'll be here—and I'll be so old—*

She washed the last bite of pancake down with coffee and made room on the counter for mixing bread. She was getting out her bread-mixing pan when she realized she had forgotten to tell Roy to get kerosene. Oh well, it would be a good excuse to let Carl drive to Ziegler's store.

She had hoped to get the kitchen floor scrubbed before Gertie came. But all she had done, after bathing and feeding the baby, was to wash the dishes, when little Clyde burst through the door, followed by Gertie carrying chubby little Earl.

She patted Gertie's fresh young cheek, hugged little Clyde, and reached for Earl. "My land! He weighs a ton compared to Jeanie. And look at him smile! I'll be so glad when—"

Gertie was already holding Jeanie. "Oh Ma, she's so tiny! So thin! Have you weighed her? Is she still throwing up as much? And her cheeks are so rough and red!"

Emma sagged into the rocker. "Well, she isn't throwing up quite as much—not like when she was in the hospital. Why, they'd prop up a bottle with a big hole in the nipple, and she'd gulp it down, throw it up, and cry another four hours."

"You think Emmie could hear her?"

Emma took off little Earl's sweater and shrugged. "I don't know. The times I was there they had her anywhere there was an empty bed. Couldn't put her in the nursery 'cause she wasn't born there, you know."

Gertie shook her head. "Emmie was so happy—so proud of her." She blinked back tears. "Ma, if you want to work in the garden, I'll take over in here."

12

Emma nodded. "Oh, yes! I'd like to get started. Carl helped me scratch in a few peas last week, but it's high time I got the root crops in." She put on her straw hat and stuck a steel knitting needle through the hat and in the pug on the back of her head.

Little by little, the tension spring inside her unwound as she hoed and planted. *Good to know Gertie's with the baby. Those boys don't know what to do when she cries.* Emma straightened up and rubbed her tired back. Leaves were almost full-grown now; the lilacs were budding. Surely the violets were in bloom down by the river. No time to pick them to put on the graves for Decoration Day this year. She'd put that pink geranium on Emmie's grave and transplant some creeping myrtle from Al's. Then she'd plant a red carnation on his, as she had done all five years. Five years! And now "Papa" had his little Emmie with him.

She tore open an envelope of carrot seeds. Such a short while, it seemed, since last spring when Emmie was still teaching in Kennan, all excited about teaching closer to home in the fall. In love with Ed, yes, but not quite ready to get married at nineteen. But they had. Quickly. Quietly. She had taught until Christmas and then they had moved her bedroom set and cedar chest to Phillips where his brother Charles, and his wife Sodonia, lived. Emmie was happy to be in the same house with her friend and former schoolmate, Sodonia, and didn't mind the tiny rooms. In summer they'd buy a house in town near Edward's garage.

"The baby will be born the middle of April," she had said. "Oh, Mama, it was just that one time—" And she had cried and cried.

But the baby had come March 31 at home, and in the midst of a blizzard, and four days later they had loaded Emmie on a stretcher into the baggage car of the train. The fever she had developed the second day was raging by the time she was admitted to Ashland General Hospital.

Emma started when Hank slammed the garden gate. "Gert says dinner's ready."

The fragrance of fresh-baked bread greeted her. She pulled the knitting needle out of her hat and hung it up while little Clyde clambered at her feet, pointing to her head. She picked him up. "What is it, honey? What do you want to tell Grammy?"

Gertie came over, potato masher in hand. "Tell Mommie. What are you trying to say?"

He examined Emma's head with a pudgy finger.

"I don't know—I took off my hat—"

"Oh, Ma! He's looking for the hole in your head! He thinks you stuck the knitting needle through your head!"

They laughed and his little lip trembled. Emma hugged him close. "Oh, sweetheart, we weren't laughing at you!" She took the needle and stuck it through her pug. "See! Here's where it goes!"

They were still laughing when the boys trooped in.

Roy grinned. "Sure good to hear someone laughing around here again."

"You know," Emma said as she cleared the table after dinner, "this was the first meal I haven't had to force down."

Gertie laughed. "Must have been my cooking. Couldn't have been the exercise."

Emma reached for her straw hat.

"Ma, you look awfully tired. Why don't you take a little nap before you go back out?"

"Well, I suppose I could—for a little while. I am tired. Not long though. Want to hoe the cabbage patch and set out those plants."

It was two-thirty when Emma's sleep-creased face appeared at the kitchen doorway. Gertie looked up from cleaning lamps and smiled. "Now don't fuss, Ma. You needed that sleep."

Emma sat down heavily. "I thought it was morning—that I'd slept a whole night."

Gertie pulled the coffeepot over to the front stove lid. "I'm just about done, and then we can have a cup of coffee."

"But there wasn't enough kerosene. I forgot . . ."

"Oh, I found a little more in the barn," Gertie said, replacing the last chimney. "Don't worry! I shook the lanterns. There's enough in them for tonight."

Emma poured steaming hot coffee while Gertie put away the lamps. Jeanie's bottle was warming in the teakettle. Emma stared at it. Last Christmas morning, she had opened the big heavy package from Emmie and Ed and lifted that teakettle out—all shiny and bright. Ed had looked more like an elated schoolboy than a twenty-nine-year-old car salesman. "Best Christmas of my whole life," he had insisted.

"Look who was waking up," Gertie said, holding baby Jeanie's rough little cheek close to hers. "She's been a good girl today."

Emma sighed. "I hope she sleeps tonight."

Gertie shook a few drops of milk on her wrist and sat down. "Bless her little heart, she's starved! Oh, I didn't get to tell you. I went to see Minnie Sunday."

"How is she?"

"Miserable. Sure hope that baby isn't late. She wanted to hear all about—everything. It's still hard for her to believe Emmie's gone. After all, we saw her laid out and went to the funeral and everything. I told her how pretty Emmie looked in that pink chiffon dress and about the pink rosebuds Ed had me pin between the puffs of the casket lining and how she looked like she was just sleeping and how

15

beautifully Roger Evans sang. Minnie cried a lot, but she needed to get it out.''

Emma nodded. "Yes. That was good. Ella and I were talking the other day about how hard it would be for Minnie because she couldn't be there.'' Emma bit her lip. "Worst part for me is waking up in the morning. For just a moment I feel good and then I remember—and I want to think I dreamed it all. It was different when your Papa died. He was sick so long and suffered so much.''

"I know. I don't think I grieved for him till months later—after I forgot about the suffering a little.''

"Had a letter from Ed. Poor man. He says if it wasn't for the baby, he wouldn't want to live.''

"Think he'll take her, if he gets married again?''

"No. He told me he promised Emmie he never would. She wanted *me* to raise her.''

Gertie caught her breath. "Then she really did realize— She didn't let on the last time I saw her. When I came she was coughing hard and the nurse asked me to wait outside in the hall. When I went in she was propped up, smiling, and she said, 'Gee, Gert, that dress looks good on you!' And later she talked about making a little dress for Jeanie out of her lavender voile with the white embroidery because it was tearing under the arms.'' Gertie blinked hard.

"The day I took the baby home—that was only five days before she died—,'' Emma said, "one of the nurses told me they'd hear her crying at night. But all she said to me was, 'You took good care of all of us and I know you'll take good care of her.' I left her with the baby a few minutes before we left.'' Emma's voice broke. "I just couldn't stand it—I think I knew then, but I didn't want to believe it.''

Gertie put the baby down and gathered Emma in her arms. "Oh, Ma. I try not to be mad at God.''

"I know. I know. I don't understand, but I know I love

16

God and I know He loves us. Right now I can't think beyond that."

CHAPTER 2

WOULDN'T FEEL SO TIRED, Emma thought as she put potatoes on to fry the next morning, *if I wasn't used to sleeping straight through.* She hadn't tried to count how many times she had been up with the baby that night. "Feel eighty-five instead of fifty-five," she muttered, rubbing her back. "Didn't think I'd be this sore from gardening yesterday."

The gray eastern sky reminded her she'd have to dry diapers on the back porch if it didn't clear up. The diaper pile was getting mighty low.

She shook the baby's bottle and put it back in the teakettle, grateful for every quiet moment.

It wouldn't be quiet long. Little Clyde was bouncing on the bed upstairs. Just thinking of Gertie's going home today brought tears to her eyes. She'd miss Gertie's companionship more than her help—though the help was certainly appreciated.

She put on a smile when Gertie and the children came

downstairs. "You go up and wake Uncle Henny," she told Clyde. "Tell him to get up *right now!*"

Sunbeams gilded the porch posts by the time breakfast was over. It would be a beautiful washday, the women decided, and recruited Henny to carry pail after pail of water from the pump by the kitchen door to fill the big copper boiler and two washtubs.

While the water heated, Gertie bathed the babies.

"Should we weigh Jean, Ma?"

"Oh, yes! I've been wanting to do that."

She lugged the heavy old scale in from the milk separator room and lined the scoop with a blanket.

While Gertie's hand hovered over the baby's tummy, she moved the weight until it balanced. "Seven pounds, fifteen ounces," she proclaimed. "Almost eight pounds."

Gertie picked up the crying baby, blanket and all. "Only seven ounces more than when she was born, and she's almost two months old!"

"I know. But she was only seven pounds when I brought her home. Let's see; that's almost three weeks ago. Think something's wrong with her?"

Gertie frowned. "I don't know. She *is* gaining. Why don't we see how she does in another week and, then, if she isn't gaining faster, maybe you should take her to Dr. McKinnon. He might be able to give you something to put on that rash, too."

Emma nodded. "I'll try real hard to get her to eat more."

The diapers and tiny clothes had been boiled, washed, and rinsed. Emma gave a diaper a smart snap before hanging it out. *Never thought these old lines would hold diapers again.*

When she came in, Gertie was gathering Clyde's and Earl's toys and clothes. Roy had said he would take her home after dinner.

Emma started to tell Gertie how good it had been to have her home but had to stop in midsentence to dry her eyes with her apron. "Silly goose! I didn't think I was going to cry. Just hate to have you leave, but I know you have a lot of work to do, too." Gertie slipped her arm around Emma's shoulders.

"Nonsense! I can stay another day. Joe won't be home until Friday. We'll work on our garden Saturday."

"Oh! Could you? You just don't know—" and she started to cry again.

"I'll stay on one condition."

"What's that?"

Gertie wagged her finger under Emma's nose. "That you take a nap after dinner."

Emma sat down in the rocker and heaved a sigh. "I won't even argue."

They were feeding the babies later that afternoon when Gertie said, "Are you planning to take the baby out Decoration Day? It's next week, you know."

Emma shook her head. "I don't think so. She cries so much I probably wouldn't hear the speaker anyway, and, even if that rash is gone, I don't think it would be good for her."

Gertie sighed. "I wish you could go. It's the one time of the year the whole community gets together and you can see old friends."

"Guess I'd just as soon not see them right now. By next year it won't hurt as much to talk about Emmie. But now—"

"I dread talking with people right now, too, even though they mean well. But I want to see all the family. I don't get to see Mamie and Al and George and Sadie as often as I'd like. Mamie said the little boys have new white sailor suits, and Ruby had a new blue dress for Decoration Day."

Emma laughed. "She'll be scrubbing grass stains off

20

Art's suit the next day for sure and Paul's won't have a spot. Like night and day—those two boys."

"That they are! Mamie says Ruby is talking a blue streak these days."

"Oh, she's a smart little one for two."

"Wait till you see all those little cousins," Gertie said to Clyde as he snuggled up against her.

"Well," said Emma, "he is blessed with relatives. With thirteen children—twelve, now, with Emmie gone—my cup runneth over with grandchildren! What will we do when John, Roy, Carl, and Hank have kids?"

Clyde ran off, Buckley at his heels. A moment later he was back, crying and pointing to the dog cowering under the dining room table.

Gertie examined Clyde and yelled over his crying, "I don't see any sign of a bite or even a scratch!"

Emma stalked into the dining room, crouched down, and shook her finger in the little dog's face. "What's the matter with you! Did you growl at him? Outside with you! Get!"

Tail between his legs, Buckley scooted out the door.

"Don't know what's ailin' that dog. Could he be jealous of the baby?"

"Maybe. He's been the whole cheese around here for a long while." She chuckled. "He should know he's the only dog that was ever allowed in this house."

The day Gertie went home Emma put the baby on the comforter and Buckley came out of his favorite spot under the table and curled up on a corner.

Good. Emma said to herself. *Maybe he won't be so jealous if he can share her comforter.*

At noon Carl brought in the mail and sat down to read the *Youth's Companion.* "What's the matter with Buckley?" he yelled to Emma. "He's almost shakin' his fur off."

21

Emma came to see. "Well, I never saw him do that. Isn't cold today. Wonder if something scared him. He's getting old, you know."

Emma put the baby on her comforter, Buckley curled up on a corner, in the dining room while they ate in the kitchen.

"She's starting to roll around," Emma told the boys. "Yesterday I found her on the bare floor."

They talked about Buckley and his shaking spells. Roy had seen him do that, too.

"What we need," Roy said, reaching for the potato bowl," is a farm dog—a collie we can train to chase cows for us. Ran my feet off after those dumb heifers this morning."

That would be a good idea, Emma thought later as she lowered a stack of plates into the dishpan. *Anything to make the boys' work easier*.

The baby's sharp cry startled her and she ran to the dining room. Buckley had backed off his corner of the comforter where the baby had rolled, but his fur bristled up and his teeth were bared.

Emma snatched the baby and glowered at him. "Why, you cross old dog, you! Don't you dare hurt this baby. Get outside now!"

She held the door open and watched him slink outside. *Little dog, I'm afraid your days are numbered*, she sighed.

CHAPTER 3

WHEN DECORATION DAY DAWNED CLOUDLESS, Emma almost changed her mind about going to the community gathering at the cemetery. But the baby's screaming as she was bathed convinced Emma to stay home. She would have a little holiday anyway—at least she wouldn't have to cook. The ladies at the Norwegian Lutheran church next to the cemetery always served dinner, and the American Legion sold ice cream cones.

After the boys had gone, she swept the kitchen and fixed the baby's milk for the day, put on a sweater, and took her knitting out to the porch swing.

By now the program at Wilson School would be over and they'd be marching to the cemetery. The firing squad would fire a salute over the graves, little ones would hold their ears, and babies would let out startled cries. There'd be tears as parents placed flags on the graves of sons and, surely, prayers of thanks for the safe return of others. Once they were home, it was easy to forget to be thankful. She needed to stop right now and thank God for her son Eddie's safety.

Lord, I sure don't understand why Eddie didn't get home before his papa died, but I do thank you for bringing him home. Don't know what he's doing today in Eau Galle, if they have a parade or anything, but he's no doubt thinking of his dead buddies and of those awful times. Father, please take those bad memories away so they don't keep him from being the man You want him to be. Much as we wanted him home when Al was dying, I wonder if maybe you wanted to spare his seeing his papa that way. Now he remembers him well and strong. You always know best.

How they had tried to get Ed back! The Red Cross had tried to help, but he had come home on the very last troopship, and Papa had been gone six weeks by then. Funny how "Al" had become "Papa" to her. Reckon she'd called him Papa so long in front of the children that she just thought of him as Papa now—even in her most intimate memories of him.

She shook herself back to the present. No use thinking about those years. She'd not waste these precious quiet moments.

Good to sit still. Good to rest. Lawn looks nice. Glad Henny cut it yesterday. Shadows sharp.

The scent of lilacs propelled her memory back five years. "Why don't you bring some lilacs in here?" Papa would say when he'd see them swaying at the window. They would bring them in and a few minutes later, he'd say, "Get those stinkin' things out of here. Can't stand that sweet smell." The next day he'd say the same thing and they'd go through it all again.

Will not think about Papa now. Got to think about the baby, all the spring work, how to help the boys—Oh, dear! The baby already. She put down her knitting with a sigh and went to heat a bottle.

A bit chilly outside. She tied the pink ribbon of the little cap Emmie had crocheted, wrapped the baby in a blanket, and took her out to the swing.

She tried to sing as she fed Jeanie, but no matter what song she tried, it made her want to cry.

Right now, people would be walking through the cemetery, admiring plants and flowers. The Verlager lot would look nice with the pink geranium and the red carnation and the grass freshly cut. Maybe some would stop at Emmie's grave and say, "What a shame," or "She was such a special girl."

Even before she was born, Emmie had been special. Emma had hardly been able to believe she was really having another baby when she was expecting Emmie. Three years earlier, when she had had the stillborn child and the infection, the doctor had said she would never have another baby. She had felt so guilty—like she was responsible for that baby's being born dead. Little Roy was getting big enough that she could leave him to help outside again and Ella—poor little girl! She had suffered, too, thinking God was punishing *her* because she had been angry about another baby coming. Ella had actually thought *she* was responsible for the baby's death. But Emma hadn't known until a long while later that Ella had felt that way—only after she had confessed her guilty feelings.

So Emmie had been especially precious. Since all the baby things had been given away, Emmie had had new ones. It had been a thrill to dress her in soft new little sacques.

And now, this baby. So different. So difficult. *Never had a baby who cried like this,* she said to herself. *And this rash—never can tell if it's better or worse. If I only knew what to do for her. I think I should take her to the doctor one day and the next it looks better and I wait again.*

She'd better lay her down again and get some more knitting done. The boys had worn out so many socks last winter she'd have to knit like everything to replace them by fall.

No sooner had she come back out and sat down than the baby cried again.

"What's the use?" she muttered as she tied the little cap back on and took the baby back outside.

She wanted to relax and enjoy looking up at the gleaming white clouds and the deep green of the pine and spruce trees against the blue sky, but her eyes kept straying to the dandelions along the driveway. She didn't even dare look at the garden where she knew weeds all but hid the vegetables.

She wished Ella and the family would stop on their way home. But it would be chore time and they'd have to get right home.

Wish I had one of those ice cream cones, she thought. *I'm just like a kid when it comes to ice cream cones.*

She was so absorbed in her own thoughts that she wasn't aware of a car driving into the driveway until it sped past the end of the porch and on to the rear of the house. She had only a brief glimpse but it looked like her sister, Gustie, sitting next to the driver.

Oh, my goodness! Could it possibly be Gustie and one of her boys? She hurried through the house to the back door. There was no one she'd rather see than her light-hearted sister. If anyone knew what Emma had been through, Gustie did. Her home in Ashland had been their refuge those five weeks when they'd visited Emmie in the hospital. Driving over a hundred miles on muddy spring roads hadn't been easy.

Emma flung open the door. "Gustie! It *is* you! I'm so glad. Come in! Come in! Luke! Bless you, boy. Did you have a good trip?"

After hugging Emma, Gustie shed her coat and reached for the baby. "Still a skinny little thing, aren't ya! Aw,

26

never mind. Some day you'll be fat like your Aunt Gustie. How's she been, Emma?''

Emma shook her head. ''She cries so much—and her skin—''

''Looks like eczema to me.''

''Eczema?''

Gustie shrugged. ''Don't know exactly what it is, but one of mine had it. The doctor gave me some salve to put on it and said it would go away. And it did.''

Sometime after two that morning Gustie came downstairs and held out her arms for the crying baby. ''Here. Let me take her. You go get some sleep.''

''Oh, no! You go back to bed. I wouldn't sleep anyway.''

''Try it!'' Gustie ordered, extracting the baby from Emma's arms.

And Emma did sleep—straight through till the boys got up.

The next day, Emma poured out her grief and frustration with the crying baby, Henny's rebelliousness, the never-ending work, and much more. ''Every now and then, in my mind's eye, I see Emmie walking in, all bright-eyed and strong, and saying, 'Mama, I'll take her now.' ''

Gustie, usually ready with a bright quip, didn't say a word.

''Why is taking care of this baby such a chore for me?'' she asked Gustie directly after receiving no answer for a long while. ''After rearing thirteen, you'd think it would be easy.''

''For one thing,'' Gustie answered, ''you're forgetting that many of those babies were taken care of with the help of older children. Minnie and Gertie took care of Henny, almost more than you did, after he was weaned.''

Emma sighed. "That's another thing! Can't get used to those bottles. All that washing and boiling and mixing! And it takes her forever to eat, and I sit there looking at all I have to do."

"Prop the bottle up and go to work then! She needs to be held—but not all the time!"

Again, that night, Gustie took her turn with the baby so Emma could sleep.

When it was time for them to leave, Emma thanked Luke profusely for bringing his mother. Gustie hugged Emma hard and long. At the doorway Gustie turned and said, "Emma, I just don't know how you're going to do it—"

Emma nodded solemnly in agreement.

But Gustie continued, "—love that baby and feel sorry for yourself at the same time." And she strode out to the car, leaving Emma open-mouthed.

Stunned, Emma turned to her work. *Feeling sorry for myself I am not! All I did was tell her how things are!*

Emma got out the big aluminum bread-mixing pan and made a nest of flour. "Humph!" she muttered. "She can go back to her nice quiet house. Easy for her!"

She added potato, water, shortening, salt, and the yeast she had set the night before, then stirred in the flour with a wooden spoon.

Indignation rose in her and burst like bubbles in a pot of thick oatmeal. Up, up those thoughts came until she spat them out—inaudibly, of course, but with vehemence nonetheless.

Spoiled! Pampered! That's what Gustie was! How those boys cater to her! Hadn't she said that all she had to do was tell Willie what she wanted planted where, and it was done? Can just see Henny doing that! No chickens. No separator to wash—just a cozy little house in town, with a bathroom. And here I thought she'd understand!

28

She sifted flour over the spoon, rubbed off the soft dough, and began to knead the bread. She sniffed and wiped a tear from her cheek with her flour-sprinkled arm, as she ignored the crying baby.

Oh, Gustie had been helpful. That she could say. Why not? Wasn't hard to help for a few hours or days.

On and on the ugly thoughts came.

By dinner time Carl took one look at her and said, "Ma, what's the matter with you?"

She pretended she didn't hear him.

"One of you could hold that baby," she snapped as she dished up dinner. She was aware that they exchanged glances and shrugged. Roy picked up little Jean.

After dinner she tried to lie down for a few minutes but, as soon as she did, the baby started to fuss. "Oh, what's the use?" she grumbled and picked her up to pace back and forth the length of the house.

She laid the baby down and let her cry while she put the bread in pans, but her jaws ached with tension and she felt trembly inside. "I can't do it!" she sobbed as she covered the loaves with a clean dish towel. She sat down in the rocker, apron over her face, and cried softly.

"Father, I'm so miserable! Help me!"

The thought came, *Go back to the beginning.*

"The beginning?"

What did Gustie say?

"She said, 'I don't know how you're going to do it.'" And I thought she did understand how hard it is for me. But then she went on—'love that baby and feel sorry for yourself at the same time.'"

Can you, Emma, love the baby and feel sorry for yourself at the same time?

She dried her eyes and tiptoed to the bedroom where the baby now slept and picked up her old leather-bound Bible.

29

She turned to the slip of lined paper that marked that special spot in First Corinthians.

Lips moving, she read, "Charity suffereth long, and is kind; charity envieth not." *O Lord, I do envy Gustie.* She read on and phrases jumped out at her. ". . . is not easily provoked . . . beareth all things, believeth all things, hopeth all things, endureth all things . . ."

Endureth . . . endureth . . . beareth . . . hopeth . . . is kind . . .

She staggered back to the kitchen rocker. Charity is the same as love, she knew, since Reverend Fischer had explained it to the ladies' group on Sunday afternoon.

"O Lord," she groaned. "I see that I *can't* do both at the same time. It all seems so unfair! But where did You ever say that life would be 'fair'? I know I can't keep on this way. I've got to make up my mind. What will it be?"

She closed her eyes and words echoed: *beareth . . . endureth . . . is kind . . . is kind . . . suffereth long . . . beareth . . .*

"All those ugly thoughts. I'm so ashamed. I don't want to think like that! Forgive me. Help me. I want to love like that, but I don't know how I can do it. You'll have to help me."

The baby started to cry again, and, instead of the usual tight resentful feeling, came caring warmth—like she used to feel with her own helpless little ones.

Emma rushed to her, picked her up, and crooned, "It's all right. It's all right. Grammy loves you. Grammy loves you."

A week later, Ella said, "Ma, you seem different—better. What's happened?"

"It's hard to explain, but the truth is that I've stopped feeling sorry for myself, and has it ever helped! Now, when the baby cries, instead of feeling cross, I feel sorry for *her*. I even forget about all the work when I take care of her!"

30

"I'm so glad. I didn't know how to help you."

"Oh, those thoughts come sometimes, but when I begin to think I can't do it, I remember He has helped me so far and He will keep on helping me. I used to get so impatient when I fed her 'cause it took her so long. Now I feel like I've really accomplished something when I get her to take four ounces."

Little Jeanie was beginning to seem like her baby. One day when the boys laughed at the baby and said she was "all mouth" when she yawned, Emma scolded them until Roy said, "All right, Mother Hen, don't ruffle your feathers. We won't laugh at your chick."

Then one day, after her bottle, the baby smiled—a genuine I-know-you-smile. Emma hugged her close. "Oh, you little sweetheart! It's so good to see you smile!"

Soon after that she made another discovery; the baby didn't cry while the phonograph was playing. Emma only wished records were ten times longer. Changing records every two or three minutes kept her running. At mealtimes, when the baby was fussy, the boys took turns hopping up to change records.

"When we get some extra money," Emma said as they listened to "Where The Silvery Colorado Wends Its Way," "Let's get a new record. I think I've heard them all a hundred times. Maybe we could get another hymn by Henry Burr."

Even the rash didn't concern Emma as much since Gustie had given her hope it would go away—until the baby's father came one Sunday. Jeanie's little face was raw and rough. Though he tried to hide his distress, Emma saw tears in Ed's eyes.

She tried to explain what Gustie had said, but it didn't sound convincing—even to her.

"Maybe you should take her to Dr. McKinnon," Ed said, and added quickly, "But you do as you see fit."

Emma dabbed at the weepy spots that cracked when the baby cried or smiled and said she thought that was a good idea. She had never felt the need to take her children to the doctor—but this one was different.

Ed brought a crib and a canvas swing for the baby. "She'll be able to look around and be more content," he said.

When Emma took little Jeanie to visit Dr. McKinnon, he indeed confirmed Gustie's diagnosis.

"Well, well. Infantile eczema," he announced. "Usually lasts until they're through cutting teeth. Could be longer, but don't worry about it. It will go away."

"Will she have scars? Her cheeks crack open and bleed."

He shook his head. "Never saw anyone become scarred. Here. Try this in her milk instead of what you're using." He handed her a can. "And here's some salve that might help a little."

After Emma reported the doctor's diagnosis to Edward, she hung up the phone and said to Roy, "It just isn't like raising one that's born to you. It's like working with someone always looking over your shoulder."

She longed to say more but she couldn't expect a twenty-one-year-old to understand how it felt to face all those years of child-rearing while one's strength gradually ebbed away.

As she undressed, the apprehension she had felt as she was talking to Roy grew until it became cold fear. *What if she didn't live till Jeanie could be on her own?*

Far into the night she tried to imagine little Jeanie in one after the other of her children's homes, and each time she simply didn't fit. "Father," she groaned, "please keep me strong and well until she doesn't need me anymore."

CHAPTER 4

EMMA HADN'T EVEN FINISHED WASHING the breakfast dishes when Gertie called to report: "Minnie had a little boy last night! His first name is John, but I don't know if they've decided on a middle name."

"Oh, I'm glad. How is Minnie? Everything go all right?"

"Oh, she's fine. Tired, but things went well. Dr. McKinnon was there in plenty of time. I'm glad Joe was home to be with our two when Nels called for me to come over."

"Bet Amy's excited. How about Georgie? I worry about that little fellow. She has such a time getting him to eat."

Gertie chuckled. "No trouble with Rosie, though. It was late. I didn't get to see the kids when Nels told them."

"Oh, I weighed Jeanie yesterday morning. Eight pounds, eight ounces! She *is* gaining!"

"Good! Let's see—that's fifteen ounces since we weighed her three weeks ago."

"The formula must agree with her. Doesn't seem to be helping her skin though. I was hoping it would clear up.

33

Oh, did I tell you about the trouble we're having with Buckley? He gets shaking spells and he's so snappy. I hate to get rid of him, but I'm afraid he might bite the baby.''

"What a shame. He's been such a good dog—until now. But I know what you mean. Remember when I was there—how he startled Clyde?''

Emma sighed. "Yes, that wasn't like him. We'll just have to watch him and see how he behaves.''

Two days later, they were eating breakfast, while the baby and Buckley shared the comforter. Suddenly she screamed and Buckley disappeared under the table. Jeanie's skin wasn't broken, but there were indentations of his teeth on her little arm. She was more frightened than injured.

Emma's voice shook: "That does it! I can't watch that dog all the time and we can't risk having her bitten. Anyway, he could be sick. He's got to be shot—today.''

"I can't do it.'' Emma said to Henny, who was hunched over his plate, "You'll have to take care of him. He's old and sick, but we can't let him hurt the baby.''

Awhile later when Emma decided it was time to give Buckley a good-by pat, both Henny and the dog were gone. "Just as well,'' she sighed. "No sense getting all riled up. Has to be done.''

She assured herself that Henny was a good shot. He'd shot more wildlife than the other two boys put together. He'd have no trouble.

When he came back she heard him walk through the kitchen and dining room to put the gun away on the stairway rack. She'd see how things had gone when he came back through the kitchen.

But he didn't come back. Instead, she heard sobs.

Drying her hands on her apron as she went, she hurried to the stairway. She squeezed down beside him on the stairs where he sat, head in hands.

34

"Oh, Henny!" She put her arm around his heaving shoulders.

"Ma—the first shot—it just wounded him. He whined and crawled toward me for help." Henny sobbed some more and Emma cried with him. "But I couldn't—I couldn't help him—I hadda finish him fast."

Still sobbing, he turned and buried his head, little-boy-like, in her shoulder. "I'll never forget that look. He couldn't believe I had hurt him. Oh, Ma! Why'd *I* hafta do it?"

Emma held him close, saying, "I'm sorry. I'm so sorry." For that moment, in their mutual grief, their life-circles converged. He had actually turned *to* her instead of away as he usually did. She longed to keep this fast-becoming-a-stranger son close.

"Oh, Henny, Henny, I wish it hadn't had to be this way. I wish you hadn't had to do it, but you *will* forget."

He shook his head. "I'll *never* forget." He sat up and pulled a red print handkerchief out of his pocket and blew his nose and dried his tears. "Ma . . . you won't tell Roy and Carl I cried, will you?"

She squeezed his shoulder. "Of course I won't."

Her heart ached for him all day. That night, at the dinner table, he avoided her eyes and ate very little.

She slipped her arm around his shoulders when he came in to get a drink, but he pulled away and threw the dipper back in the water pail, ignoring the water that splashed out on the floor, and stalked out.

O Father—what have I done to that boy? Help him! Help him!

She prayed for him again as she walked the floor with the baby that night.

The next morning Henny was more sullen than ever and most of her thoughts were of him—until Carl dashed in with

35

the mail yelling, "Guess what! Fred and Helen are coming home!"

Emma grabbed the letter. "When?"

"First week in August!"

"Think Ed and Connie can get home, too?" Roy asked when he came in.

"Hope so. But maybe not. Mail carriers can't take time off from work like that."

"I don't even remember what Fred looks like," Henny mumbled.

Emma's fork stopped in midair. "Why, I suppose you don't. He hasn't been home since Papa died five years ago. You were only nine then and there was so much commotion. He'd been off cooking in lumber camps since you were little. Never really lived at home after you were born. He must seem more like an uncle to you than a brother. It would be different if he lived close by like Ella and Al. They were gone, too, but you saw them all the time."

"I remember Fred being kinda quiet," Carl said.

Emma chuckled. "Oh, he can talk plenty. But he never did talk loud. Wasn't real strong when he was a boy. Tall, but not muscular like the others. Guess that's why he'd end up helping around the house more than the other boys. But he was no sissy!" Emma added quickly. "It was just that he didn't mind doing housework. Why, he could bake better than us women. I remember one time we were over at Ella's and she had baked sugar cookies but there wasn't much sugar or shortening in them, mostly flour, and they were awfully thick. You know sugar and shortening were precious in those days, and she tried to make it go as far as possible. Well, Fred picked up one of those fat cookies, looked at it a minute and said, 'Ella, when I bake cookies, I bake cookies. When I bake biscuits, I bake biscuits.' "

Carl grinned. "Did she get mad at him?"

"Oh, I don't think so. We all had a good laugh, that's all."

Later, when she talked to Ella, Emma asked her if she remembered that incident.

"Oh, I certainly do! Think of it every time I make rolled cookies. Say Ma, the kids were asking how old Kermit is and I couldn't remember if he's Harold's age or Myrtle's."

"Hmmm, let's see. He was born before Papa died—the same year as Paul and Amy—so he's six—a little younger than Harold and older than Myrtle. I was trying to remember what day Everett was born. I've forgotten so much of what happened this spring."

"I think it was March 16. I know he's about two weeks older than Jeanie."

"And about twice as big, I bet."

When Emma talked to Gertie she said, "Oh, won't it be fun to see all those babies together—Earl and Glen and Everett and Jeanie and little Johnny—and all those two-year-olds—Grace and Norma and Shirley Emma and Rose and Clyde."

"And Dorothy and Ruby aren't much older," Gertie added. "Want me to start calling everyone and planning a reunion for the Sunday they'll be home?"

"Oh, would you? I've been thinking about that, but I've got so much to do! I'm so glad they're coming, but I don't know how I'll get this house in shape by then. Never did get the curtains washed this spring—."

That night Emma's thoughts whirled far into the night.

A few days later dinner was waiting for Carl to come home from Ziegler's store.

"Well. About time!" Emma muttered as Carl drove in.

The porch door slammed and he yelled, "Ma! Come out here a minute."

37

What on earth? He sure sounded excited.

She bustled out and saw the boys crouching down around something. A puppy!

Carl stepped aside to allow her to get closer. "The Millers said we can have him. They're movin' and can't take him along. He's about three months old and he's real smart and he'll be a good cow dog 'cause he's a collie—with a little German Shepherd in him and his name's Colonel! How you like him?"

Emma patted his smooth brown head and ruffled his white chest. "Nice white collar." He wiggled and tried to lick her hand but didn't jump up on her.

"Look at his tail!" Roy said. "Perpetual motion!"

"Colonel is a good name for him," Emma said. "Always thought of a colonel being dignified, and he is. He doesn't jump all over a person like some crazy pups."

A few feet away Hank held out his hand, palm up. "Come here, boy, come on!"

Colonel trotted over and Hank gathered the fluffy little fellow in his arms.

Haven't seen him grin like that for days, Emma thought. "Carl, go get Jeanie."

Carl held her down so the dog could see her and, tail wagging furiously, he sniffed her little feet as she stared and waved her little arms and squealed.

"Well," Emma said, taking Jeanie from Carl, "looks like they might get along. One thing's sure. He'll stay outside. All the time." She shook her finger at them. "I don't want him to set one foot in the house! You hear?"

Three heads nodded.

"Well, come on. Let's eat." she said and led the way in.

That night the last thing Emma saw in her mind's eye was Henny—grinning.

CHAPTER 5

"I CAN'T GET OVER how much I've accomplished these last few days," Emma said as she scurried around the kitchen the day Gertie came to help her wash curtains. "Doesn't it feel good to be excited about something?"

Gertie dumped a load of crisply starched curtains on the table. "Guess that's what they call being 'motivated.' There isn't much we can't do if we want to badly enough."

"Hmmm. I guess that's right." Emma laughed. "Now all I have to do is figure out how to keep wanting to—when we're not having company, that is. I get things done fast when I see them through someone else's eyes . . . Look at the gladiolus along the driveway. They should be in bloom by the time Fred and Helen come. I'd like to put a nice bouquet up in their room and another one in the front room."

"Or right here on the kitchen table," suggested Gertie. "That's where we are most of the time."

"That's right. Might as well put them where we can see

39

them. I'm going to get those vases and wash them right away while I think of it. They've been standing in the cellar since last fall.''

Emma came back with two tall narrow vases, one milky green, one clear glass. She washed and polished them, using a little brush on the many-pointed star on the bottom of the clear one.

It was nice to have Gertie to talk and work with, but Earl was creeping and getting into everything.

"At least there's no slop pail for him to get into like when you children were little," Emma said. "I'll never forget how happy I was when Papa told me he was going to put in a sink with a drain when we built this kitchen. But when I saw the men digging and digging that long, deep ditch all the way to the hillside I felt awfully guilty. All that work just so I wouldn't have to carry a slop pail!"

Gertie picked up a flatiron from the stove with the detachable handle, wet her finger, and quickly touched the bottom. It didn't sizzle so she tried another one. "You were never sorry you had it, I bet!"

Emma sprinkled water on a curtain with a snap of her fingers and rolled it tight. "Oh, of course not. You know, Papa even talked about putting in running water but when he got sick—don't matter. After carrying water from the river and the spring all those years, it's luxury enough to have the pump right by the back door."

Gertie changed irons and started another curtain while Emma slid the finished one on a rod. "Mmm. Smells nice and fresh. I'm glad you talked me into doing the upstairs ones, too. Another thing we should do is iron a set of sheets for their bed." Emma held up her hand. "Don't say it! I know. You *always* iron your sheets. Well, that's fine—long as you have the energy, but I've been lucky to get pillowcases ironed lately. Person has to make choices. I can't

40

do all those things and have enough energy left to be good-natured with the boys and the baby, so I live with wrinkles."

Gertie sighed. "I know. But it's so nice to get into a smooth bed."

Emma arranged the gathers on the curtain and said, "Someday someone's going to invent cloth that doesn't have to be ironed!"

"Oh, Ma! Who ever heard of such a thing?"

"Well, I don't know why not. The Bible says, 'Ye have not because you ask not.' Well, I'm going to ask God to help someone invent that kind of cloth. Lots of things I'd rather do than iron."

The day after Gertie left, Emma hummed and worked and thought it was good that Fred and Helen were coming now instead of right after Emmie died. *I was having such a hard time getting used to mothering that little one,* she thought, *that I wouldn't have been civil company.*

It still wasn't easy. The baby woke several times every night and cried often during the day. The eczema took a lot of care, too, but now Emma's heart was in that care. A recent dream had confirmed Emma's new feelings: Emmie had come back—like she had been on a trip somewhere. Immediately Emma's joy had been smothered by the thought, *Oh, dear! She'll take Jeanie away!*

I feel like a juggler, Emma thought the morning of the day Fred and Helen were to arrive. *Have to keep up the regular work and still get things ready for company.* She knew that the juggling would continue all the while they were there, too. If only the baby would be content.

One blessing about being this busy, she realized late in the day, was that she hadn't had time to get impatient waiting for them to come. They had written that they would take the ferry from Muskegon to Milwaukee, stay there overnight, and get an early start from Milwaukee in the morning. If they didn't have car trouble they should arrive around six, Roy had said. He had driven a new car back from Milwaukee for Edward once. He should know.

The boys decided to do the milking before supper but they each managed to slip in and grab bread and jelly before they went to do chores, Emma noticed.

At six, Emma turned the chicken again. It was a beautiful golden brown. Now, if only they would come before it dried out, she thought as she looked up the road again.

Any minute. Any minute now they would be right here—right in front of her eyes. Five years since she'd seen them. Would Fred look much older? He had turned thirty-five the last day of May. There were so many things to ask Helen. What was their neighborhood like? Were the people friendly? Would little Kermit be a lot like Fred at that age or more like Helen's family? And the baby! Jolly little fellow, they had written.

Oh! If only they'd come. Right now!

Emma changed her apron, smoothed her hair, put up a clean roller towel, and washed some spots off the mirror with the soiled one.

Six-thirty. Maybe they had had car trouble.

The baby began crying and Emma changed her and put her in her swing, staring out the pantry window again.

She checked the table again and poked at the chicken. *Pickles!* She'd run down to the cellar and get a jar of Fred's favorite dills.

When she came back up, Fred was out of the car stretching his long legs and arms. She caught her breath. *My, he looks like Papa,* she said to herself.

In a few long strides, Fred's arms were wrapped around her and then he was holding her at arm's length. "You look good, Ma. I didn't know—"

42

"Oh, I'm fine. So *good* to see you, boy!"

Then she was trying to greet Helen, Kermit, and the baby all at the same time. She patted Kermit's blond head and said, "You're going to be tall just like your Daddy." He smiled and ran to pet Colonel.

Helen hugged her with one arm as she balanced baby Everett on the other. "Mother! How are you?"

Emma held out her arms as Helen passed Everett to her. "What a little honey you are!" she said, and kissed his smooth little cheek. Under her breath she murmured, "Wished Jeanie's cheek was as smooth."

Then "Come in! Come in!" Emma urged. "Fred, the boys are still in the barn. The baby's in her swing, Helen."

In a moment Helen had little Jeanie in her arms. "Why, you're a little lady now, aren't you?"

That evening, while Helen put the little boys to bed, Emma sat down with Fred who was still sipping coffee. "I know how hard it must be for you to realize Emmie's gone. We were right here through it all; yet at times I think it can't possibly be true—that she'll be back."

"To me she was still a little girl," Fred said, struggling to control his voice. "She was only fourteen when I saw her last. I could hardly picture her teaching—much less married and a mother." He cleared his throat. "We knew how she must have suffered—I don't mean only with her illness this spring—I mean getting married and having to quit teaching and all." He shook his head. "That was the last thing I ever expected to happen to Emmie."

Emma traced the tablecloth pattern with the tip of a spoon handle.

"Yes. She suffered. She always wanted to do right and she was so sorry. I suppose there will be some who will always remember that wrong, but those who knew her well knew how contrite she was and that she had asked for and accepted the Lord's forgiveness.'' Emma brushed a few crumbs from the table into her hand and rubbed them into a fine powder in her fingers as she talked.

''That's all past, Ma. What's important now is that little one. Must be hard for you to start all over with a baby again, but she will be a comfort to you when the boys get married and have their own families. You'll have her to live for.''

Emma reached across the table and clasped Fred's hand, but her eyes avoided his. ''I get so scared,'' she whispered. ''What if something happened to me?''

They could hear Helen coming down the stairs. Emma met Fred's eyes briefly and withdrew her hand from his reassuring grasp.

''Mother! How thoughtful of you to take the time to put the gladiolus in our room. They're beautiful!''

Emma's face flushed. ''I was hoping a few more would be in bloom. Maybe tomorrow there'll be more and we can put them here on the table. Now, about tomorrow—church is at half past nine. I'll take care of the little ones so you can go.''

Helen put her hand on Emma's shoulder. ''No. We've talked it over and we know you haven't been able to get to church very often and we want you to go. I'll take care of the children and Fred will go with you.''

One didn't argue with Helen, so Emma found herself in church the next morning.

It was good to hear Fred's voice singing ''Rock of Ages'' across the aisle. It didn't usually bother Emma to sit on the women's side of the church, but today she wished she were sitting with her sons.

Like that of a willful child, her mind wandered during the sermon to all the things she must do when she got home. Time and time again she tried to force her thoughts to the words the pastor was saying, but off they would go again.

After the sermon she took out her offering money and held it as she prayed—eyes open so she wouldn't miss the *Klinglebointen* when Gust Zielke extended its long handle down the pew. It had long ago lost the little bell that had hung on the bottom of the velvet bag.

O Father, she prayed silently, *I'm sorry my mind wandered. Forgive me. And I'm sorry I let work keep me from you. I don't spend nearly enough time with You. Remind me. And today—help me not to miss one single thing that I should do or say. You know I want to be a blessing to them—like that vir-virtuous woman in Proverbs. Don't let me ever say or do anything that would bring shame to them. And, Lord, help me to be loving, even when I get tired.*

She dropped her money in and let the words of the last verse of "I Am Trusting Thee, Lord Jesus" flow through her mind. Clara Hoffman saw that the collection wasn't finished and played one more verse.

> I am trusting Thee, Lord Jesus;
> > Never let me fall.
> I am trusting Thee forever
> > And for all.

Lord, I am trusting You and I know no one ever trusted You in vain.

She realized that the thoughts that had plagued her all through the sermon were gone. She sighed. Now, when it was time to go home, her mind was settled on the Lord. *Help me remember how blessed it is to be with You,* she prayed quickly as Reverend Fischer gave the benediction.

Then friends were gathering all around her.

"Oh, Emma! How *are* you?"

"How's the baby? Is she still crying as much?"

45

"Don't know how you manage. I just couldn't start with a little one again."

"You take care of yourself. You look awfully tired."

They were barely home before the cars began coming. Emma stood on the well platform and tried to talk to everyone as they arrived.

Henry, Ella, and the children piled out of the car and Ella bustled across the yard, arms loaded with bowls of food and followed by the four boys, each carrying more bundles. Grace and Myrtle ran ahead into the house.

"Ma?" Ella called over her shoulder, "the boys want to go swimming down in 'Grandma's swimming hole.' Should I let them go now or stay and eat first?"

"Oh, let 'em go now," Emma said with a wave of her hand. "Run along, boys. Who knows when we'll be ready to eat?" She tweaked Harold's nose as he grinned up at her. "You'll be good and hungry when you get back."

The boys ran off hooting and hollering, Henny right behind them.

Emma turned to Henry standing beside her. "Always makes me laugh: 'Grandma's swimming hole!' Never swam in my life. We girls weren't allowed to swim. But Gustie—she did." Emma chuckled. "Wasn't much Gustie didn't try."

Then she turned to greet Al and Mamie and Paul, Art and Ruby, George and Sadie and Dorothy, Norma and baby Glen, as they trooped in with dishes of food.

She was about to go check on the coffee when John and Ed, Jeanie's dad, came in. John gave her a one-armed hug and said, "Here's some lemons for lemonade." He shrugged. "I didn't know what to bring."

Emma greeted Gertie and Joe and the boys, and Helen

came out holding Everett. Gertie and Helen exchanged babies and Emma smiled at all the exclamations.

"He's got so much hair, Gert!"

"Look at all those teeth. He's smiling to show them off!"

"Come and see Sadie and George's Glen," Helen said. "They're in the house. "All these little boys! Ed's little Allison should be here. Sounds like he's a smart little guy. Connie wrote that he was walking at ten months and saying quite a few words."

Gertie held the screen door open for Helen. "Poor little Jeanie with all these boys! Maybe Connie and Sadie will have girls. They're both expecting," she whispered.

"And here's the new one!" Emma said, as Nels and Minnie drove in. Carefully, Minnie climbed out of the car carrying five-week-old Johnny. Little George clung to her skirt, two middle fingers in his mouth.

Amy took little Rosie by the hand and ran off, and Nels was left to carry in the food. "Hello, Mother," he said, as he hurried into the house. Emma knew he would find an inconspicuous spot and stay there the rest of the day. His severe spine curvature had certainly not kept Minnie from being attracted to him, and Emma had hoped their marriage would give him new confidence. But he seemed to be more withdrawn than ever this year. *What a shame*, she thought. *That man probably has more intelligence and ability than all the rest of us put together*. There seemed to be no limit to what he could do when it came to anything electrical or mechanical.

Emma started to go in again, but waited when she saw Len and Nora drive in. She gave Elaine and Goldie quick hugs as they dashed by and watched Nora step gracefully out of the car. As always, Emma admired her slim ankles and her glowing dark red hair. If Nora weren't such a loving person, Emma might have been uncomfortable with her dignified city ways.

"Are we the last ones?" Len called across the yard.

"You might be," she called back. "Ed and Connie can't come, and everyone else is here."

When Len greeted her, he added, "John's been doing real well lately. Hasn't missed work for a long while."

"Oh, I'm glad," she said with a quick glance behind her. "Hope you can keep him working with you awhile. I thought he'd bring Esther."

Len shrugged. "Oh, they've had another lovers' quarrel," he said as he went on toward the house.

"Nora! I'm so glad you could come!"

"Oh, Grandma! Isn't it a lovely day? I can't wait to see everyone."

Shirley Emma clung to her when Nora said, "Honey, say hello to Grandma Verlager." She turned to Emma. "She's been talking about seeing her 'other' Grandma all week."

"How is your mother?"

"She's fine. She asked me to greet you for her."

Later, while everyone was sitting around on the lawn, Emma tried to etch all the faces in her memory. All eight sons had Papa's dimple in the chin and large ears but, like a variation of the same musical theme, each one was different. She watched Len throw back his head and laugh, while Al merely chuckled.

If only Ed and Connie could be here—and Emmie. A pang of grief shot through her. Right now she'd have been cuddling Jean and talking young-mother talk with the others.

Emma swallowed hard and shook her head. She would not think of Emmie now. Now was the time to take in all that was going on. Might be a long time before they'd all be together again like this.

It didn't bother her that she wasn't involved in conversation. She needed these precious moments to store away these scenes, these sounds. A wave of gratitude swept over her. No conflict among them. Papa would have been so happy. So proud. She could see how he'd stride around teasing the girls and talking with the boys and glancing her way as if to say, "Aren't they great, Emma?"

Quickly she switched off the scene in her mind's eye. No time to think of what might have been. Only time to see what *is*.

She smiled at the children flitting here and there like colorful birds. She needn't have been concerned about them having a good time. Now and then someone cried over a bump or a little squabble started, but alert parents brought speedy silence.

Young Colonel trotted along reveling in all the attention—especially from Shirley Emma, who squealed with delight when he tried to lick her.

Len heard her and came to see what was happening. He came over to Emma grinning. "She told me, 'He yicks me 'cause he yikes me!' "

"She is such a little dolly." Emma said. "Love to hear her talk."

Len looked up at the sun. "We'd better get some pictures while the light is good. I'll get Al."

Eventually everyone was rounded up before Al's camera—all except Nels, who stayed under the box elder tree.

Later, when everyone was back talking in groups here and there, Emma heard loud laughter and went to investigate.

"Come, sit down!" Mamie called. "The men are telling hunting stories."

Emma sat down and winked at Mamie and smiled as they watched Carl's hands—talking as much as his mouth.

49

"John! He's the guy that has the luck! Remember a couple years ago when there wasn't any snow? A whole bunch of us—John an' me an' Roy an' Hank—Ed musta been there—and you were there, Len. We'd made drive after drive all day down by that old burning. About four we quit. No snow for tracking—hadn't seen a thing all day. We started headin' for home feelin' pretty disgusted. Some of us decided to follow that old right-of-way, but John and me an' Len an' Hank took the trail along the edge of the timber. Well, John changed his mind and wanted to cut across the swamp to meet the other guys so we said, 'Go ahead. We ain't goin' that way.' "

John grinned and nodded.

"Well, when we got almost to camp ten, we heard shooting east of us," Carl continued, "so we headed in that direction."

"Yeah," Roy said, "And we heard the shots and started toward them, too."

Carl shook his finger at Roy. "We saw you guys coming but couldn't figure out who'd done the shooting. Then we got up on a little knoll and there was John down by an old rampike—what's he doing? Dressin' out a nice buck!"

John grinned. "Eighteen-pointer!"

"Only deer anyone saw all day," Len said. "That's luck!"

Ed was taking it all in, Emma noticed. It was good to see him laugh.

"Say, Carl," he said, "I heard something about a skunk getting you on your confirmation day but never heard the whole story. Didn't you know better than to get near one?"

Even the mention of that incident made those who had been present chuckle, and they urged Carl to tell Ed how it happened.

"Well, it was like this. Skunk hides were bringin' a

pretty good price that year and Hank an' I figured if we could catch a couple pair, we could start breedin' them. We built some pens down by the river so they'd be ready when we caught some. We'd read that if you grab a skunk by the tail and lift its feet off the ground, it can't spray. Well, it worked. We caught a couple that way. But that Sunday I ran out quick to check the traps, and I had a nice big feller. I got him out and was hiking down toward the pens when that stinker bit my little finger! I was holdin' him in my right hand and I had a stick in my left hand, so I just hauled off and hit him one on the nose so he'd let go my finger.''

Carl was laughing so hard by that time he had to stop before he could go on. "He let go all right! Not only my finger, but with his spray apparatus, too! My face was about a foot and a half away so I got it good! I couldn't see. I couldn't breath. I could hear the river about a hundred feet away, and I stumbled and crawled down there and dove in. I washed and washed and finally I could see enough to get home.''

At that point Gertie controlled her laughter long enough to take over. "We had him scrub and scrub, and then we doused him with talcum powder and perfume—''

Carl wrinkled his nose. "Whew! That stuff was worse than the skunk!''

"And we went to church,'' Gertie continued.

"Shortest confirmation service in history!'' Roy added.

All too soon the women began gathering up children and dishes and Emma was saying goodby over and over again. *Not so hard with those living close*, she thought. But how would she ever tell Fred and Helen and the little boys good-by in the morning?

That night, as she prepared for bed, she could still see and hear fragments of the day's happenings—Minnie's

51

chatter, the children's laughter, the men's voices. She could see mothers and their babies, Sadie's pale face and straight back contrasted with Ella's rosy cheeks and curves, the tenderness in Edward's eyes when he held little Jeanie, Shirley Emma's delight over Colonel, giggly little girls and Fred, like her, taking it all in—trying to preserve it all.

Tomorrow they'd get in that little black Ford and drive away. Quick tears came to her eyes. Would it be five years again before she saw them?

For a moment she didn't think she could stand to let them go. The little boys—they'd be different people when she saw them again.

The next morning the frying pan blurred through tears as she fried potatoes. She ducked into the pantry and dried her eyes on her apron and tried to ignore her aching throat.

All the while she helped them load the car, she was cheery, but when Fred held her close, sobs blocked all the words she had planned to say.

And then they were turning around in the driveway, waving, calling goodby.

The four of them watched until the car disappeared over the hill. Then, without speaking, each went his own direction to search for a way back to everyday life.

CHAPTER 6

No matter which way Emma turned on the morning Fred and Helen left, she saw work—and more work. Given a choice she would have crept back to bed, but she couldn't ignore the baby's crying, or the low diaper pile, or the house that looked like over forty people had reveled there the day before.

She'd work hard this morning, she decided, but after dinner she'd take a nap. Hadn't her friends at church Sunday remarked about how tired she looked and cautioned her to take care of herself and admitted that they couldn't do what she was doing?

At dinner time she struggled to keep her eyes open.

"Threshers are heading this way," Roy said at the table. "Should be here by Friday."

Emma groaned inwardly: *Oh, no*! A threshing crew to feed in a few days. That she didn't need right now. Instead of napping, she'd have to get out and pick the beans, tomatoes, and cucumbers. She'd have Henny pick up windfall apples even if he did grumble.

Many of the tomatoes were overripe. She'd have to can them right away.

Down in the dark cellar she picked out an armload of jars and started up the stairs. One dropped. She wanted to leave the shattered glass right there—simply ignore it—but she made herself go down and sweep it up.

She'd need boiling water for washing jars and scalding tomatoes. Better get a fire going. She reached in the wood-box for kindling and wood. Empty. No sense yelling for Henny. He was down in the orchard—or at least he was supposed to be. She'd have to get her own wood.

The baby was screaming when Emma came in with an armload, but she took time to kindle the fire before she picked her up.

For a while the baby was content in her swing but then she squirmed and fussed, and Emma put her on the floor where she continued to be fussy.

By the time Emma hung up the dishpan that night, she was staggering tired. If the boys wanted to stay up past dark, they could light the lamp themselves. She was going to bed to end this miserable day.

"Ma! I'm outta socks!" she heard Henny yell the first thing the next morning.

"Go look in Carl's or Roy's drawers," she yelled back.

"Roy's last pair," he said, waving them when he came downstairs. "Carl's out, too."

Oh, dear, she'd planned to wash today anyway, but where were all the socks? She had washed them all last week. One glance at the mending basket solved that mystery. *Should have darned socks while I visited last week,* she chided herself.

She didn't even get near the string beans or cucumbers,

much less the apples. It had taken her all morning to do the washing and keep the baby quiet.

"Could be threshing here by Friday," Roy announced at the table.

He put the last of the butter on his potatoes. "Frank Knorn'll be at Scheller's tomorrow. We gotta help there and the next day at Hank and Ella's." He handed the empty butter dish to Emma.

She scowled. "Go get it yourself. Won't hurt you."

Carl untangled his long legs from under the table and headed toward the cellar, looking back over his shoulder.

"Well, what're you starin' at me for? No reason you can't wait on yourselves a little around here," she snapped.

After dishes were done she decided to call Gertie before she started canning tomatoes.

"Oh, Ma! I was going to call you. I feel kinda lonesome today. You rested up after all the company?"

"Oh, I guess so. But I just can't get caught up with the work and now the threshing crew'll be here Friday."

"I wish I could help you but with Earl getting into everything, I'm more bother than I'm help."

"Thanks, Gertie," Emma sighed. "Just wish the boys would be a little more helpful—have some idea what it's like for me."

"We've spoiled them by waiting on them hand and foot, haven't we?" she asked.

They talked about Sunday but when Emma went back to work, she felt more sorry for herself and more lonesome than ever.

She worked all afternoon at the tomatoes, except for the time it took to take in the clothes and fold them. She didn't even start the beans or cucumbers. Better not sprinkle the starched clothes, she reminded herself. No telling when she'd get time to iron them.

As she set the table for supper, she grumbled to herself, "When am I supposed to dress fryers and bake apple pies and darn socks and finish canning and scrub these dirty floors and still keep the baby happy?"

She could see Jeanie's father as he had showed her off Sunday. "Pretty easy to be proud and beaming. He doesn't have to put up with her," she mumbled.

After supper, Henny's laughter drifted in from the back yard where he was playing ball with Byron Olafson. *All this work to do and he doesn't see a thing.*

"Henny!" she yelled, dripping dishwater across the floor in her haste, "Go close the chicken coop. It's almost dark."

"Aw, Ma."

"Aw, Ma, nothing! Do it right now before you forget. Too dark to play ball anyhow."

She stomped back in the house. *Fine time to be doing supper dishes. Bet every woman for miles around is done— especially everyone my age. They're sitting on their porch swings or in their rockers.*

"Oh well," she sighed. "I must get used to doing young-woman things with an old-woman body."

Evidently getting up on time two mornings in a row were Henny's limit. Wednesday morning Emma had to tap with the broom handle twice. She woke the baby and still he didn't come down.

When he heard her coming up the stairs, he hopped up in a hurry.

She railed at him all the while he laced his shoes.

He waited until she stopped to catch her breath and said, "You're an old crab lately. Carl and Roy say so, too," and out he ran.

"Well!" she exclaimed, hands on her hips, "So I'm an

'old crab,' am I? I'd just like to see them put up with what I have to put up with around here!"

At breakfast Roy said, "Ma, did you close the chicken coop last night?"

"I told Henny to."

Roy scowled at him across the table. "Skunk musta got in. They're still squawking down there and I think there's one missing."

There was.

"Can't depend on that boy at all," Emma muttered as she kneaded bread, the baby crying all the while.

By noon Emma was aching tired. She did get the beans canned while the baby slept but the baby woke up crying. Nothing satisfied her—swing, bottle, floor pad.

Finally Emma picked her up and gave her a good shake. "You cry, cry, cry! No matter what I do for you, you cry! You're just spoiled, that's what you are!"

The baby stared at her—eyes wide with fear—then her lip trembled and she began to sob.

Instantly, Emma's frustration and anger vanished.

"Oh, *Liebchen, Liebchen!* I'm sorry! It isn't your fault." Emma held her close, tears running under her glasses. "I'm so tired—so discouraged—"

Crying baby in her arms, she sat down in the rocker and prayed, *O Father, I'm so sorry. Forgive me again! I've been thinking about me, me, me, and feeling sorry for myself ever since Monday. Some blessing I've been to my family!* She remembered the fear in the baby's eyes and cried some more. *I don't want to be like this—help me! Please help me!*

Words floated into her mind, and she whispered them: "I can do all things through Christ which strengtheneth me."

"It's all right! It's all right!" she crooned, and the baby quieted.

She tried the swing again. The baby smiled.

57

CHAPTER 7

THAT OCTOBER MORNING Emma didn't even ask Henny to carry wash water for her. Pumping water would give her an opportunity to take deep breaths of the crisp air and to commit that blue sky to memory for the gray winter days to come.

She needed to get the pumpkins and squash in the cellar, dig the carrots and put them in sand, sort through the apples so the bad ones wouldn't spoil the rest, and wash windows—how good it would be to look out at the lawn and way up the hill through nice, clean windows instead of through all those flyspecks!

Colonel pranced at her heels while she pumped a pail of wash water, and she thought of Shirley Emma's delight with him last summer. Word had come that both Nora and little Shirley were sick. She didn't know what was wrong; surely by now they were fine again. Probably some little upset. She thought about the new little "Shirley"—Ed and Connie's baby born September 24, and hoped they'd get home in summer.

She dumped another pail and went to check on the baby. Sound asleep. A picture of her own mother came to Emma's mind.

Now I see it wasn't easy for my mother to raise Little Anne, Emma thought. *We never realized what a struggle it must have been to have a little one in the house again. I know how my mother must have grieved for my sister, Anne, and how sad she felt when Anne's husband put two in an orphanage.* A chill went through her when she remembered: Little Anne had been only thirteen when Ma died; her mother had been fifty-two when she took her.

Emma tried to enjoy the blue sky as she hung clothes, but she fought worrisome thoughts all forenoon.

Arms akimbo, she gazed out of the pantry window, wondering how an artist would paint that scene the window framed. The sky, she noticed, was many shades of blue. The woods peering up over the top of the hill she'd paint dark, dark green; the road, red-brown. The pasture—why it looked like an old gray wool comforter with holes poking out of it. One of these years, as the sod crept over them, the boulders would be completely covered.

The shine of the creek she'd paint white. She'd capture a spring garden, all neat with many rows of various shades of green. *But that wouldn't be right with the other fall colors. Have to make it all spring or all fall.* She shook her head. *Silly thinking! Me! An artist!*

A car drove up in the driveway, interrupting her imaginings. John! What on earth? He never came in the middle of the week. Had Len fired him?

He kept his head down and he walked toward her, then put his arm around her shoulder and said, "Where are the boys?"

"Oh, I really don't know where Roy and Carl are. Henny's here. Henny!" she called. "Go find the boys."

59

John waited until Henny had run toward the barn. "Ma—" His voice broke. "Little Shirley Emma's dead. Diphtheria. Nora's got it, too."

They were sitting at the table staring at coffee cups when the boys came in. John told them and they sat down in stunned silence.

The sun was low before all the family had been contacted.

The boys went to do chores and Emma remembered the diapers on the line. She had been singing—so carefree when she had pumped water this morning. Could it have been only a few hours ago?

O Father, pull Nora through, Emma prayed as she took Jeanie's diapers from the line. She dabbed her eyes with a diaper. *God, I don't know why these things happen, but I know You don't want them to. I feel like You're crying right with us. You are a God of love. I know that. I don't understand why some must die while others are spared, but please make Nora well and don't let the others get it!*

Nora. Nora with the silver-bell laugh. Nora with the fair skin and glowing red hair—dear Nora.

John went back to Phillips that night and in the morning he called and said that Nora was still in critical condition.

They would come and view Shirley Emma's little body through a window before the funeral service.

As she blew out the lamp that night, Emma thought surely this was one of the saddest days of their lives. A glimpse through the window and a brief graveside service and they were on their way home again. How she had longed to comfort Len, but fear of contagion made it necessary to stay at a distance. Nora's condition had not improved, they were told.

Father, she sighed at last, *I'm prayed out and I'm cried out. I rest in Your almighty arms.*

Each succeeding day John would call Gertie to relay the news. The report was the same for three days: Nora's condition was still critical.

They worked automatically and talked little—the boys, that is. Emma spent a great deal of the time either answering the phone or reporting Nora's condition to others.

"I feel like the whole world is holding its breath," Emma told Mamie the third day. "At least my world is. Even little Jeanie senses something's wrong. The boys don't play peek-a-boo with her or toss her around, and she sees me crying a lot. She has the saddest look on her little face."

The fourth evening, as they sat around the table, Emma said, "Surely Nora must feel all these prayers. Len, too."

"They ain't feelin' mine!" shouted Henny. "I ain't prayin' to a God who kills little kids!"

Emma was so startled she didn't get a word out before he continued.

"Why'd He let her die? He can do *anything,* can't He?"

Roy started to say something but stopped and looked questioningly at Emma.

Henny shoved his chair back, got up, and paced the floor, smacking the magazine into his palm. "That's right, ain't it? God can do anything?"

Emma laid down her knitting. "Yes. He can."

Henny's eyes blazed. "Well, then, why didn't He make her well?"

Emma cleared her throat. "You answer me something first. Does God *make* us do anything? Does He like everything we do?"

Henny stopped pacing. "No—no. But what's that got to do with it?"

"It means that He *can* do anything, but He doesn't always. He could have created us to obey Him but He didn't.

61

We can make up our minds what we want to do or believe—isn't that right?"

Henny nodded.

Roy and Carl hung on every word.

"Don't you see, boys?" Emma said, accenting her words with a knitting needle. "If He controlled us, we would automatically love Him—and what kind of love would that be? Love isn't love unless we can choose to love, is it?"

Roy and Carl nodded as Henny sat down and scowled.

"Don't see what that's got to do with Shirley Emma dyin'."

Emma sighed a long sigh and leaned her head back against the rocker. "I know it isn't simple. I don't know why God does what He does, but I know this—He is a loving God! He grieves when we don't live the way that is best for us—the way He tells us is best in His Word. Things started going wrong way back in Eden because man wanted his own way, and it's still goin' on. We can't blame God for what is caused by sin."

Henny scraped his chair back, flung the magazine on the table, and stomped off to bed, muttering, "It don't make sense to me."

Carl and Roy exchanged glances, said goodnight to Emma and went up to bed.

O Father, grief over death is hard, but grief over a hard heart is worse. Help him! Emma prayed as she undressed.

The fifth day dragged by. The boys ate supper, talking only when necessary, and went silently to do chores. .

Emma was sitting at the table sipping lukewarm coffee, the baby on her lap, banging a spoon, when the phone rang.

It was Gertie—crying and trying to talk: "She's *better!* The doctor says she's going to live!"

Emma ran down to the barn, crying and saying, "Thank-You, Lord! Thank-You, Lord!" all the way.

"Boys!" she yelled. "Nora's better! She's going to live!"

She didn't even stop to see how they responded. She had many calls to make.

CHAPTER 8

HENNY PUSHED THE Montgomery Ward catalog across the table, keeping his finger on the item he wanted Emma to see. "Look at this. It's called a 'Come-back.' Think Jeanie would like it?"

"Hmmm. 'Come-back returns when rolled,'" Emma read. She held the catalog at a different angle to catch the lamp's feeble rays. "I'm trying to see how big it is. Oh, 'three inches in diameter,' it says. She'd be able to hold it, I think. She'd like that, but where are you going to get the money? It's forty-nine cents. That's half a day's wages!"

Henny chewed his lip. "Figured I'd trap weasels. Bet I'll get a whole bunch of 'em before Christmas. One thing, though: gotta stretch 'em and ship 'em. Might not get paid in time."

Emma smiled. "When I see the weasels, I'll give you a loan."

Henny grinned. "Gotta buy your present in town so you won't see it on the order blank."

Emma, smiling, realized she had seldom seen her sullen

boy excited and thinking about someone else. There was much little boy in him yet.

But her smile vanished at the thought of Christmas and all the painful memories it would bring. She ached for Len and Nora's loss and for her own. The first Christmas after Papa was gone, they'd all tried to be cheerful—to remember the real reason for joy—but they missed him. All the Christmases since had been a struggle. The boys, too big for toys, feigned delight over handmade socks, mittens, and wristlets and the trifles they gave each other. Even putting up a tree had become more of a chore than a pleasure. Emma sighed. Maybe the baby would make a difference.

"Wait'll you see the swell tree I found," Carl announced a few days later. "Balsam, like you always want, and it's *perfect*. Think we can order some new candy cherries and beads and stuff?" He gave Jeanie's swing a push. "Wait'll you see that Christmas tree, kid!"

Emma smiled as she watched Jeanie giggle at the silly faces Carl was making. Then he sent her swing sailing through the doorway. Yes. The baby *would* make a difference. But Emma still dreaded the empty space no one but Emmie could fill.

As Emma put *Pfeffernuesse* in baking pans just a few days before Christmas, she could suddenly see the boys and Emmie bantering as they had trimmed the tree last year, and grief, like an unexpected ocean wave, caught her off-balance. How would she get through Christmas without Emmie's bubbling laughter?

The afternoon of Christmas Eve, Carl set the tree in the old stand Papa had made of crossed two-by-fours, ready to bring in the house after the church program. Emma planned to take the baby to church.

"Baby going bye-bye," Emma told her as she dressed her and sang:

65

Hang up the baby's stocking
Be sure and don't forget
For the dear little dimpled darling
Has never seen Christmas yet.

Roy came in, smiled, and winked and they sang the next verse together:

I told her all about it
She opened her big blue eyes.
I'm sure she understood it
'Cause she looked so cunning and wise.

Carl watched with a grin on his face.

That night, as the huge tree was lighted with a candle attached to a long pole, Jeanie's little eyes grew round. No crying tonight, and though she wiggled as the children spoke, she watched every move and sat quietly as they sang.

After the service, folks clustered around and remarked about how she was growing and patted her shiny hair. Her response was a little smile and a big yawn. Emma laughed. "Hope she's that sleepy when we get home."

"Oh, go ahead and get the tree in," Emma told the boys as she undressed Jeanie. "She doesn't know what's going on." But they refused to bring it in until she was safely in bed. It must be a complete surprise, they insisted.

When Emma came out of the bedroom, the tree was placed and they were turning it this way and that to find the best side. What had looked perfect in the woods looked less than perfect in the house. "Oh, it *is* a lovely tree," Emma assured Carl as Henny and Roy teasingly pointed out flaws.

Then she polished fragrant delicious apples and piled them high in her cut-glass bowl as she did each year. Last year Emmie had explained to Ed, "We've had apples in that bowl every Christmas as long as I can remember."

He had squeezed her hand and replied, "I like that. Let's do things like that—start our own traditions—next year when we have our own home."

But, Emma thought bitterly, they didn't even have one Christmas in their own home.

"Hey, Ma," Carl called, interrupting her thoughts, "is this candle far enough away from that branch?"

"I don't think so." She got up and helped him find a better place for the candle holder. Then she brought out the box she had hidden and put hard candy, chocolate drops, peanut brittle, and mixed nuts in bowls, warning as she did so that they were only to sample them tonight.

The boys brought their gifts for little Jeanie—unwrapped so she could see them right away—and tissue-paper-wrapped packages for each other.

Henny placed the red-and-blue Come-back well in front of the large roly-poly Carl had bought and frowned at the fluffy brown Teddy bear Roy was giving her. "Wonder if she'll even see it," he muttered.

Emma brought out a rag doll she had sewn during Jeanie's nap times, and thought of the many rag dolls she had made through the years.

"Now, don't let her see anything in the morning until we get the candles lit," Carl reminded Emma.

Like little children reasoning that the sooner they got to bed the sooner morning would come, the boys trooped up to bed.

Emma refilled the candy and nut bowls. She hadn't had the heart to limit them to samples. One more stick of wood in each stove and her day's work was done.

She sat down a moment and took deep breaths of the balsam fragrance. But tonight it evoked grief, not happy memories. She felt it growing, gathering deep within her and she quickly prayed, *Father, help me! Don't let me spoil the day for the boys—and Ed when he comes. And Father, comfort Len and Nora. Help them through tomorrow.*

Before she blew out the lamp, she tucked the covers higher around Jeanie's little shoulders and kissed her rough little forehead. "God bless this baby," she murmured. "Such a little honey."

No problem getting Henny up this morning, Emma thought as she tied her old pink flannel robe around her. She heard the boys tiptoeing around and she could smell the sulphur from the matches used to light the candles.

Before she brought Jeanie out, she peeked around the doorway. "Merry Christmas, boys! You ready?"

Carl scurried in from the kitchen and Emma lifted Jeanie out of her crib and wrapped a blanket around her. "It's Christmas Day, honey! Let's go see—"

She snuggled against Emma's shoulder. "She isn't quite ready to wake up yet," Emma explained. But when Emma turned toward the tree, up came Jeanie's little head and her eyes flew open.

Emma tore her eyes away from the baby's face to watch the grinning boys and then put Jeanie down on the floor, blanket and all.

Henny was beside the baby in an instant, demonstrating the Come-back. She waved her little arms and made happy sounds and tried to grab it when it rolled back to her. Then she spied the roly-poly and Carl quickly showed her how to set it wobbling. Roy stood, arms folded, watching them. He caught Emma's eye, winked and smiled. Jeanie would find the Teddy bear and the rag doll eventually.

Ed came well before noon and enlisted the boys' help in unloading the car.

"What's Daddy's little girl got? Show Daddy!" Ed said, looking down at her playing with her toys. "Pick her up for me, will you Roy?"

Oh dear! Emma thought. *He's having trouble with his back again.* At times she forgot that he wore a heavy brace. His back had been broken while he was in the army and a portion of leg bone had been grafted into his spine.

"Wait till you see what Daddy brought you!" he said. "Carl—that big box. Want to open it?"

"A rocking horse!" Emma exclaimed. Though it was made for a tiny child—a bent-wood circle enclosed the seat—Jeanie was so tiny she couldn't reach the footboard or the handles that protruded from the horse's head.

"We'll fix that," Emma said as she tucked a blanket behind Jeanie. "Won't be long before she'll be rocking herself."

"Those," said Ed, pointing to two large flat boxes, "are yours, Mother."

Emma sat down and opened one. It was a large portrait in an oval frame. "Oh, Ed! Thank-you! My, weren't you handsome in uniform!"

Henny whistled. "That frame real gold?"

Ed smiled. "Gold leaf, I guess." He rubbed his hands together nervously as he waited for Emma to open the second box.

She reached for it, her heart thumping. Surely it was a portrait of Emmie. *Help me, Father,* she prayed silently as she lifted the top off the box.

"Oh, Emmie!" she said, her voice breaking at the sight of the almost life-sized image.

Ed haltingly explained that it had been made from Emmie's class picture. "Wanted one of her smiling," he said. "She was rarely so sober. But we couldn't find another picture clear enough to enlarge."

69

"It's beautiful, Ed. You know I'll treasure them both. Such a beautiful frame," she added, fingering the intricate design.

The boys took a quick look and disappeared. *Oh, dear,* she thought. *They didn't need such a vivid reminder. I've got to think of some way to lift everyone's spirits.*

But before she could think of anything, Al and Mamie and the children arrived. "Thank-You, Lord," Emma whispered, as she went to welcome them.

They were hardly in the house when George walked in with a grin on his face. "Guess what we got for Christmas?" he asked the children.

"A b-i-g sled," little Art guessed, stretching his arms as wide as they would go.

"Nope!" George said, tossing Art in the air. "We got a brand-new baby girl. Her name is Ardis."

That evening Emma leaned back and closed her eyes. Quiet. So quiet. Only an occasional snap of the fire and the clock ticking. The boys had gone to bed but she needed to relive the day—Christmas, 1924. She smiled as she remembered the baby's astonishment—candles reflected in her eyes—and Henny and Carl down on the floor with her. And Ed, so delighted with Jeanie in her rocking horse. *Hope that little horse brings many minutes of peace—when she grows into it. But what a shock it was to see Emmie's face! It'll be comforting to look at that nice clear likeness someday,* but now—*thank goodness Al and Mamie and the children and George had come when they had.*

Her smile returned when she remembered George's radiant face—and little Art with his outstretched arms.

"Father, thank-You," she whispered. "The day went well. Only that one rough spot. But I'm sad because we didn't celebrate Your birthday, Jesus, the way I'd have liked to. We thought about ourselves, not You. I'm sorry,

70

and I promise next year, with Your help, to make Christmas a day that will please You. I want to teach little Jeanie all about You. I want her to love You. Please let me be with her until she doesn't need me anymore. And Father, help me be a blessing to my whole family. That's really what I want most of all.''

CHAPTER 9

EMMA BUTTONED THE LAST BUTTON on Jeanie's little shoes, stuck the buttonhook in the washstand drawer, and let her see herself in the mirror. "Look at that big girl! A whole year old today!" Emma kissed her. "And you know what? You've got the nicest, smoothest little cheek. Now we'll go put on your new dress your daddy sent you so you'll look pretty when Auntie Gertie and the boys come."

As Gertie entered, she exclaimed, "Look at her face! She's all smooth!"

Emma beamed. "Couldn't imagine that a few weeks ago. Not a sign of a scar, either. She does have some spots behind her knees and in her elbows, but that's not so bad."

"I brought my camera," Gertie said. "Let's take the kids' pictures while they're still clean and the sun is high."

Emma carried Jeanie out and stood her up in a sunny spot but she plopped down on the grass. Clyde and Earl raced around and she tried to creep after them. "Gert! Just take it with her sitting down or she'll be a mess!"

Gertie snapped several pictures and they watched the little ones play awhile on the damp grass.

"Can you remember the lawn ever greening out like this by the end of March? Doesn't seem possible that last year at this time we were having a blizzard."

Emma sighed. "A lot of things don't seem possible. That morning when Ed called and said that the baby had come, I could just see us going up there to visit them and how proud Emmie'd be . . ."

Gertie put her arm around Emma's shoulder as they walked toward the house. "It's been a hard year. This one will be easier."

Before the afternoon was over, Mamie and Al and their children and Ella and Henry and the girls had come, too. Emma rushed around, seeing that everyone had a piece of birthday cake, catching snatches of conversation about "creation" and "evolution" and the governor of Tennessee, but she couldn't piece it all together.

Al explained: "Seems there are teachers who teach that man came from apes instead of being created by God. The governor of Tennessee has just signed a bill making it unlawful for a teacher in that state to teach anything but the Bible's version of creation."

"Well! I should hope so! I hope every state passes a law like that." Emma said, loud enough to attract everyone's attention.

Al shook his head. "Looks like we can expect a lot more of this evolution teaching. Lots of people would rather believe Darwin's theories than the Bible."

"Well, land's sakes! All they have to do is look around them and they can see all this didn't happen by chance. Can't imagine anyone believing a thing like that."

For several days that conversation haunted Emma. What kind of a world would these little ones be living in if such ideas grew? But each time, before she thought herself into a dither, she cut off the fearful thoughts with a whispered prayer, "Father, take care of these little ones. I trust You!"

By May, when Jeanie was able to toddle along with Emma, she worked in the yard remembering what Gertie had said that this year would be easier. She agreed—until she had chased Jeanie down the driveway several times.

As she worked she kept up a running monologue: "That's bark from the tree. Ick! Don't put it in your mouth! Oh, look here! An angleworm. Put out your hand. Look at him wiggle!"

She had almost forgotten what it was like to see the world through a little one's eyes. She picked a dandelion to hand to Jeanie—but she was gone. "Why that little rascal! How could she disappear so fast?"

Calling as she walked, Emma searched the west side of the house, behind the lilac bush at the corner of the house, behind the rosebushes—and then she heard a high little voice calling from the front of the house, "Ma! Ma!" just like the boys would call her.

She found her by the big old honeysuckle bush—her left foot stuck between its low branches. She wasn't crying—just yelling, "Ma! Ma!"

Emma couldn't help laughing as she extricated Jeanie's little foot. She'd have fun telling the boys about it at suppertime.

One day, about the middle of June, Mamie called and invited Emma to come over the afternoon of Al's birthday, June 21. "How would it be if Al comes and gets you about one and you spend the afternoon with us and the boys come over for supper? We so seldom get a chance to visit."

That day, as she shut the kitchen door behind her, Emma felt guilty leaving all the work and going visiting but, she reminded herself, it was important to spend time with other members of her family, too.

Emma could almost smell the coffee perking as she thought of that cozy green house. It was always pleasant to visit with Mamie. In spite of much trouble with her stomach, both before and after surgery, Mamie was rarely without a smile and didn't have to look hard to find a reason to giggle with the children like a schoolgirl. It made Emma feel good just to think about being there.

Al sat down with the women to have a cup of coffee, "If anyone wants me, they'll come to the house," he said. "Never thought the time would come when blacksmithing would be a dying trade, but I see it coming."

Emma's brow furrowed. "Oh, dear! What will you do? Get more cows?"

Al shook his head. "No. Think I might try the city— Muskegon, maybe. No sense sittin' and scowlin' at the cars going by. Might as well go to work makin' 'em."

Mamie poured coffee without comment, but Emma knew she'd hate to leave her elderly parents who lived a few miles away.

"Oh, I've got news," Emma said brightly. "John and Esther are getting married next month. John asked Roy to be his best man."

Al grunted. "Sure hope they get along better after they're married than they have before."

"Now, Al," Mamie chided in her soft Norwegian accent. "Those were just lovers' quarrels."

Emma sighed. "I hope so. Esther simply isn't a happy person."

Mamie leaned close to Emma. "Where is the wedding to be? Will we all be invited?"

Emma shook her head. "John said they'll be married in the parsonage. *I'm* not even invited."

Mamie put her hand on Emma's. "Oh, I didn't know."

The screen door slammed, a welcome diversion. The boys dashed in, yelling, "Grandma! Wanna pick strawberries? There's lots of 'em."

Emma hugged Art with one arm; Paul, with the other. "I sure would—if you'll help watch Jeanie."

Mamie gave each one a tin cup and followed them out: "We can't have Al's birthday cake without wild strawberries, now can we?"

"Oh! I should say there's lot of 'em!" Emma exclaimed when they reached the edge of the woods across the driveway. She picked a stem with four brilliant red berries and twirled it in her fingers. "There's enough for a million shortcakes."

Paul gave Jeanie a berry. She put it in her mouth, squeezed her eyes shut and shivered before running away.

Emma straightened her back to watch Al hike toward the blacksmith shop. "I should have realized that, with everyone buying cars, there won't be as much horseshoeing. But there'll always be work horses!"

Mamie shook her head. "Al says it won't be many years till farmers will be using tractors in the fields instead of horses."

Emma laughed. "Oh, that boy! Whoever heard of such a thing?"

"Well, August Johnson has had a tractor for several years, and so has Edgar Weiland."

"Yes, I guess I heard that, but I thought they just used them to haul things. I didn't think tractors would be used in fields like horses. I'm way behind, I guess. Always so busy with my own work I don't pay attention to what's going on in the world. Sometimes I guess I don't want to because I don't like to see things change. I don't even want to *think* about you moving to the city."

They picked berries a few minutes in silence and then Mamie straightened up and said, "Look at little Jeanie playing with the children. She's no baby!"

Emma nodded and said pensively. "No, but there're so many years to go until she's on her own."

Mamie's smile faded. "I think I know how you feel. I was scared for Ruby when I was sick and she was just a baby."

The laughing children ran toward them. Reluctantly Emma gathered up the feelings she had been about to share and thrust them back down beyond reach. Someday there would be another opportunity to talk about them.

It seemed like summer had hardly begun when it was threshing time again. "I've come a long way since last year," Emma said to herself as she watered house plants in the bay window. "Instead of feeling overwhelmed like last year—I'm excited. I like to see the men working and joking together. And how they can eat! I'll cook a real good dinner. I don't want my boys to be ashamed of that dinner."

She smiled as she thought of the old engine coming up over the hill—putt, putt—and how that top-heavy old rig would rattle and squeak its way down to the threshing floor.

Old Frank would back the tractor up the hillside and anchor it in the same old holes and stretch that big belt from tractor to threshing rig. Load after load of oat bundles would be fed onto its conveyor to disappear into its noisy innards. Then sack after sack of grain would be drawn from its side and carried to the bin while the straw showered up into the loft through the blower pipe.

She'd take Jeanie down to watch it—if it didn't scare her.

"I was just thinking about those awful days I put myself through last year before threshing," Emma said to Gertie with a sigh, when she came to help with the cooking. "All I have to do is start feeling sorry for myself and I'm a goner."

"Oh, Ma. Everyone has a right to feel sorry for oneself now and then." Gertie laughed. "After all, I might as well. No one else does."

"But we can't be loving when we're all tied up with self-pity!"

"Who says we've got to always be loving? Oops! I hear Earl! I'll be right back."

Oh, Gert, thought Emma. *If you could only learn from my experience. But you'll have to suffer for yourself.* "Father," Emma whispered. "I fear for her. She's got to have things perfect and she works till she almost drops and then gets down and out because no one feels sorry for her. Teach her, Lord. Please help her see that old Satan just waits till we get tired to get us thinking wrong. Help me remember that, too!"

Like a stone gathering momentum as it rolls downhill, the weeks went by faster and faster until it was again Christmas preparation time. Plans revolved around Jeanie and, to their delight, she was even more responsive than the year before.

New Year's Eve, 1925, as Emma sat thinking over the past year and the holidays, she realized this was the first Christmas since Papa got sick that she had really felt happy—thanks to that little busybody.

A gust of wind set the windowpanes trembling and Emma shivered. She laid her knitting aside and put wood in both stoves. The fragrance of the tree candles still hung in the air, and the tinsel glittered as it caught the glow of the fire.

She tiptoed to the bedroom and tucked the covers close around Jeanie's neck. "Bless her little heart," she whispered. A few more months and she'd be two. Only two. At least sixteen more years to go.

Emma sat down wearily and began to take out her hairpins. *How wise God is,* she thought, *to keep the future from us. How could we ever face the future if we knew all that would happen?*

But tonight she wouldn't think about what might happen. Tonight she'd think about the happy days just past.

Tonight, when the boys left for a neighborhood party, she hadn't felt the least bit lonesome or left out. She had enjoyed solitude. There was all too little of it. "A person's in real trouble," she had often told her children, "if he can't stand his own company." Tonight she had a lot of thinking and praying to do.

She closed her eyes and watched the scenes in her mind's eye—long-legged Carl sprawled out on the floor, building block towers for Jeanie—Henny, chair tilted back on two legs, arms folded across his chest, laughing at Jeanie's antics. And her favorite scene of all, Roy holding Jeanie in the rocker, facing the lighted Christmas tree and singing Christmas carols. Each time a song ended her little hand would come up and pat his cheek and she'd say, "More! More!"

The only painful part of the holidays had been Ed's visit. He had tried to be cheerful and to win Jeanie's affection, but he was a stranger to her. When she was put into Ed's arms, she'd wiggle right down again and he'd fight back tears. No wonder his visits were becoming more widely spaced. Poor man. Emma hadn't dared ask him if the rumors John had relayed were true—that he was seeing Amanda, his childhood sweetheart. It would be hard to see someone take Emmie's place, but he was so lonely she didn't blame him. He did tell her he was having financial difficulties and may, in fact, lose the garage.

"Get so mad at myself," she had told Gertie. "I'm so self-conscious and tense when Ed comes. He has never said

79

a critical word, but I'm always afraid I'm not doing things right. It's so different from raising my own.''

The clock struck nine. Time to pray. Day after day she prayed for her family as a group and for those with special needs. But tonight she planned to pray for each one of them individually and that would take awhile. Her lips moved as she held each one—from Al to Henny—up to the Lord. She went on then to her brothers and sisters, including Little Anne, of course. She prayed for President Coolidge, for Reverend Fischer, for Dr. McKinnon, the mailman, the cream hauler, and all the neighbors.

She yawned, combed her hair, and braided it in one long braid. Dreamily she took the few long hairs from the comb and wound them around the end of the braid to secure it.

Then there's me, Lord, she continued. *I'm sure not proud of the way I lived this past year—of all the times I worried and was afraid and when I snapped at the boys and was impatient with little Jeanie. And I haven't worked as hard as I should, either. Most of the time I forgot about the patterns You gave me.*

A long while ago she had taken the last chapter of Proverbs and the thirteenth chapter of First Corinthians as her pattern.

This is the way I want to be, her heart had said years ago when she heard the minister read them. She had read them herself, too, but not often enough.

"I know some things that virtuous woman did, I can't do." (She smiled at the thought of going out and buying a field. Imagine the boys' faces if she came home and told them, "I've just bought a forty back of Hank and Ella's.")

Abruptly she brought her thoughts back in line. "I'm sorry, Lord," she whispered, but she didn't feel condemned but rather that He shared her little flight of humor.

Lord, I don't know my own heart. Do I want to be like

80

this woman so my children will praise me? I don't want to look for praise, but I do want to be a blessing to them. Oh, yes! That's what I want. But more than that, I want to be a blessing to You. I know that I can't do anything to please You in my own power but You live in me and I can do things to please You in Your power.

Tears brimmed over. *O Lord, I want to be what You want me to be. I want Your will to be my will. I want to love with Your love.*

The clock struck ten.

Father, Jesus, Holy Spirit—I love You. I trust You. I thank You for loving me. Whatever happens in 1926, I know You'll be with me.

Her words ceased then and she sat bathed in His love and peace until a blast of wind shook the windows. Automatically she put wood in the stoves, undressed and snuggled into bed—His peace still enfolding her.

CHAPTER 10

ONLY THREE PLATES on that big old table now that the holidays were over. Roy had gone back to the lumber camp, and Carl to Phillips where he worked for Len most of the winter.

Emma sighed as she finished setting the table. Work they needed. The few cows brought barely enough to buy flour, sugar, oatmeal, kerosene, and gas for the car.

"Why did I ever let Gertie and John talk me into selling so many of the cows after Papa died?" she asked herself again as she had so often. Somehow they had always convinced her to sell another one each time they needed money. Now Roy was raising all the heifer calves and the herd was increasing—slowly.

Meanwhile Emma was glad when Carl could find work and be independent, even though she missed his easygoing humor. She wholeheartedly agreed that Roy should work in camp. How else would there be money for machinery repairs or a new car? The Model T Ford Roy and Emmie had bought wouldn't run forever.

But it wasn't easy to take care of the stock with just

Henny's help. His heart was in his trap line, not the farm. Emma's concern for his spending day after day in the bitter cold with only frozen sandwiches to eat, then coming home and doing chores, alternated with wanting to shake him for not putting the farm work first.

She scowled out the window. If only he'd get home at a decent hour. The evening blue of snow and sky had given way to black and only by cupping her hands around her eyes as she pressed her face to the window could she see out at all.

Still no Henny.

She stirred the stew and moved it back on the stove.

The thought that always crouched at the fringes of her mind leaped in—*if only Papa were here!* She wouldn't have to be concerned about the cattle and chickens and the size of the woodpile or put up with Henny's grouchiness. Papa would never have stood for that.

She gave her head a sharp shake as if to banish those thoughts. Plain foolishness to think like that! Got to think about what to do right now—just the way things are!

Maybe he's had an accident. No! I will not think like that!

She'd go and start the chores even if he did get mad as he had one day last week. He had slammed into the barn yelling, "You *know* I'm comin'. Why the heck can't you wait?" He waved his arms toward the cattle, "They ain't starvin' to death!"

But she couldn't stand to think of those animals going hungry or that Molly, recently freshened, was waiting to be milked. She chuckled. Couldn't expect a man to understand. Only a woman knew the pain that delay in milking caused.

"Come on, *Liebchen*," she said as cheerily as she could, "let's go see the kitties and the sheep and the bossy cows!"

She stuck Jeanie's uncooperative arms in sleeves and stuffed her hands into mittens, then dragged her up on her lap and pulled overshoes on twisting, turning feet. As she tried to buckle the stiff, metal buckles, pain shot through her arthritic fingers and another thought, twin to the crouching one, bounced into her mind: *If it weren't for this baby—* Oh, to be able to dress herself and walk out of the house, alone, unhampered!

Jeanie's smiling little face beamed up at her and Emma's eyes misted. She slammed her mind's door and hugged the child close.

She lit the lantern, took Jeanie's hand, and picked her way over the icy bumps, accompanied by their tall shadows, saying, "Uh-huh! Uh-huh!" as Jeanie jabbered about kitties and cows.

Once inside the barn Emma sang: "Where He leads me I will follow, my dear Savior I will follow," and laughed as the big old gray mama cat escaped Jeanie's grasp.

Quickly she milked Molly and patted her flank. "There, now! That feels better, doesn't it?"

The warm barn and familiar odors eased the tension of waiting. She was glad she had started chores. She could handle most of the work herself, except for throwing down hay and a few other things, but the trouble came later when her dwindling energy supply ran out long before her housework was done and she had that little wiggle-worm in bed. Oh to be thirty again—even forty.

She was dragging hay to the cows when Henny came in, whistling. She shook her head. Never did know what mood he'd be in.

"Must have had some good catches today."

"Yep," he answered. And that was all. She wished he'd tell her about the animals the way she heard him tell Floyd Olafson when he came over. Where, she wondered, had he learned so much about nature? Certainly not from books. Oh well, at least he was in good humor tonight.

Spring brought Roy home with a variety of news, beginning with Len's phone call: "Well, Ma, we finally got a little redhead. Her name is Joy Ann." It was hard to hear because of all the crackling on the line, but Emma did make out that Nora was fine.

Another precious bit of joy came when Roy brought Mayflowers he had found in the woods for her birthday on April 18. She put them in the cut-glass toothpick holder and promised herself she'd take Jeanie up to see the spring flowers in bloom.

One sunny afternoon, about two weeks later, she took Jeanie's hand and started across the stubble field east of the house, explaining, "We're going to pick pretty flowers."

Emma set her down in the midst of the first clump of pale pink flowers. "Look, *Liebchen*. Pretty flowers!"

But Jeanie didn't stop to admire them. She was off, yelling, "More fwowers, more fwowers," each time she found another patch.

Emma smiled and let her run. Some year she'd marvel at their downy stems and delicate colors—a miracle after the lifeless cold.

"Ma! Ma! Snow!" Jeanie yelled.

Snow? *Can't be any snow left*, Emma thought as she strolled over to see.

"Oh, honey! That's not snow! That's a rock with mica in it, but it sure does sparkle like snow."

As they walked back, she took deep breaths of the cool fresh air. *I'm happy!* she said to herself. I'm really happy.

In May Ed wrote that Allison and Shirley had a new little sister named Maybelle. "My goodness, you are getting a lot of little cousins," she told Jeanie.

When, in June, Roy started talking about a new car, Emma said the old Model T would run a long while yet. She hated to see him spend all his lumbercamp money on a car. But one Sunday morning in July it refused to start when they wanted to go to church. Sitting there in that hot dusty old rig with its flopping side curtains, watching the boys probe its innards, she realized Roy was right.

And so, a few weeks later, Roy drove in with a brand-new Overland. "Ka-*oo*-ga! Ka-*oo*-ga!" He blew the horn all the way into the yard as they rushed out to see it.

"It *is* nice," Emma said as she climbed in and pulled Jeanie up beside her. She stroked the gray plush seat covers and rolled down the window.

Roy poked his head in the other window and grinned. "No more leaky roof, Ma!"

"And no more old floppy side curtains," she added.

Carl and Henny had folded back the hood, heads deep inside its inner parts, while Emma admired the shiny chrome and deep blue paint.

Roy laid the bill down on the supper table when he came in a little later. "Six hundred and forty dollars!" she exclaimed.

Carl whistled. "Good deal!"

"Sounds like an awful lot of money to me," Emma said as she set the pot roast on the table.

There was a new spring in Roy's step after he got the car, Emma noticed, and it seemed like it was always headed out the driveway.

Where those boys found the energy to go swimming at Pearson's Lake or to play ball almost every night after a hard day's work, she didn't know. But it was good to see them laughing and bantering, slicking back their hair and taking off again. Winter would come soon enough and they'd be more housebound.

Wonder if Ed will get down to see Jeanie before winter.
Sure enough, a few days later he came, bringing a friend—a
Mr. Warden—with him. He didn't stay long.

He was able to give them a little more news about John
and Esther's new baby girl, Jean. They lived in the same
rooms he and Emmie had lived in—above Charles and
Sodonia.

The baby was fine, he said, and John was about as proud
as a father could be. But when Emma asked about Esther,
he shook his head: "Don't understand that woman. She
says she's never going to have another baby. From what I
hear she didn't have an unusually difficult time."

"I felt so sorry for Ed," Emma told Gertie later. "He
wanted Jeanie to come to him, and she wouldn't go near
him. Went and sat on his friend's lap, though, little
stinker!"

"Did she sing for him?"

"Oh, yes. She sat in the rocker—rocking like everything—and sang "Let Me Call You Sweetheart" all the
way through. Ed looked so proud. And you know how the
boys have taught her the names of all the cars. They say,
'What kinds of cars does your Daddy sell, and she reels off
the whole list from Chevy to Whippet. He got a kick out of
that."

"I bet he did."

"Oh, I got over to see Sadie and George and little Owen.
I'm worried about Sadie. Her goiter seems to be bigger than
ever and she's thin and pale. George doesn't look good,
either, and he's always out of breath."

"Do you suppose it's his heart? Remember they wouldn't
take him in the army because of his heart?"

"I had forgotten that. Oh, dear."

That night, as Emma braided her hair, she thought, *I
certainly never run out of things to pray about.* She prayed

until she dozed off, woke with a start, and went to bed.

On Christmas Eve Emma dressed Jeanie in new pink sateen bloomers, the red velveteen dress Ed had sent and patent leather shoes which she shined with petroleum jelly. Emma was certain she was more nervous than Jeanie. Would she really speak the recitation she had learned in front of all those people?

When her recitation was announced, Emma whispered, "Now, go up the steps."

Her little legs were too short to walk up, so she climbed, using her hands and exposing a lot of pink bloomer—reciting as she climbed!

> It's sweet to know that Jesus
> Was once a baby, too.
> We're trying to be like Him,
> Loving and pure and true.

By the time she got to the top and turned around, she was all done.

She blinked her eyes and drew her little shoulders up, hands over her mouth, as if to say, "Well, now what do I do?"

Mrs. Semrow whispered, "Say it again."

But Jeanie whispered back, loud enough to be heard in the back row, "I did it already!"

Emma beckoned to her and she climbed down the way she had climbed up and ran to Emma's arms.

If only Emmie could have seen her, thought Emma. She realized there would be many times she would feel that way—at Jeanie's graduation from grade school, high school, college, at her wedding—or would *others* be thinking, *If only Grandma could see her?*

CHAPTER 11

"Emma, I can't get over how good you look!" Clara said, smiling up at Emma as she filled her coffee cup. They lingered at the table after New Year's Day dinner.

"Oh, I really feel like me again." Emma answered as she set the pot back on the stove. She inched her chair a bit closer to her sister-in-law, so they could hear each other over the menfolk's loud talking in the next room. "You know, I think I feel younger now than I did at fifty."

"No wonder! Those were awfully hard years when Al was sick. Took a lot out of you."

Jeanie toddled in and asked for a cookie.

She munched a few minutes and then ran off to see what the men were doing.

"She isn't a baby anymore," Clara observed.

Emma smiled. "She thinks she's so big. Says nursery rhymes galore and sings more songs than I can count—and she isn't even three. But there're so many years to go yet."

"Must be much easier for you this winter with Roy home."

"Oh, yes. Makes a world of difference. I had dreaded the winter until he said there was enough stock now that he really needed to be home. He's doing some logging right on our own place. I was so glad! Henny'd sit down there in that little shack he built way down in the timber, day in and day out. I hate having him down there alone, but he says it beats hiking those extra eight miles every day. Can't blame him."

"Does he have a dog?"

"No, but that will be next. He wants a hunting hound. At least he wouldn't be alone way down there."

"Does Carl get home weekends?"

"Usually. He's in a camp way down near Merrill, so he doesn't always make it."

"He's such a good-natured boy. Always smiling."

"I sure do miss him. He always has something to talk about. Roy is more quiet, wrapped up in his own thoughts much of the time."

"Children are all so different. Max is my companion. Don't know what I'd do without that boy. Look at him in there with Jeanie! For some reason, little ones just love him."

He was down on his hands and knees, with Jeanie clinging to his back as he played bucking bronco.

"Oh, that floor's impossible to clean!" complained Emma, taking note of the worn rug. "Need a new linoleum here in the kitchen. I was looking in the catalogs the other day. Think I'd like something besides brown and beige for a change—green, maybe."

"Isn't it nice the way they're making things more colorful? I need color, especially in winter."

"Colors do cheer a person up. Need new curtains, too. Saw some material with yellow daisies. Think that would look nice?"

Clara nodded. "Especially if you got something with green for the floor."

"Oh, I'm all full of plans! Seems so long since I had time to even look around and see what this place looks like. Now it's easier, with Jeanie trained. I feel like I could go on and on like this—keeping house for the three of us and doing for the other two whenever they come home."

One day in February Roy sat at the kitchen table scribbling figures with a short pencil. "The cream check should look pretty good by spring," he told Emma. "Six more calves and all the cows will be fresh."

"I was thinking," Emma said, scratching a pile of dirt across the worn linoleum with a stubby broom, "it would be nice to have a new linoleum—and some new curtains." She glanced sideways at him as she swept the dirt into the heavy, old black dustpan.

"We'll see," he said, frowning.

Oh, well, she thought as she washed her hands, *shouldn't expect him to get excited about a new floor and curtains.* She wouldn't mention it again until spring.

As more cows freshened, Emma began helping with milking in the evening. It was a pleasant diversion for Jeanie, too—especially when the lambs came. Emma showed her how to find clover in the hay to feed the ewes. "Clover makes nice, rich milk for the babies," she explained.

Jeanie held clumps of clover and giggled when the ewes nibbled it from her hands. Now and then she'd get exasperated because the lambs wouldn't come close enough to the side of the pen for her to pet them. Roy would tell her to be patient—that when he was done milking, he'd take one out for her.

How her little eyes lit up when he'd come and say, "All

91

right, which one do you want?'' She'd choose, and Emma and Roy would take a few minutes to enjoy watching her talk to the lamb and stroke its soft baby wool.

"Got to take a picture of her petting a lamb one of these days," Roy said.

A few days later he poked his head in the kitchen door and said, "I've got a lamb out here. Want to hand me the camera and bring Jeanie out?"

Emma hastily brushed her hair, put a clean apron on her and Roy took her picture.

"The way she loves animals, she ought to make a good farmer's wife," Emma said over her shoulder as they went back to the house.

It wasn't easy for Jeanie to understand shearing time. With Carl gone, Emma volunteered to help, but she hadn't counted on Jeanie's reaction to the struggling sheep or to their bloody spots when the shears nipped them.

She cried and begged them not to hurt the "sheepies."

"Honey, it's all right!" she tried to tell her. "See, we put salve on them and the hurt will go away. They're just scared when they kick and roll around. They aren't hurt."

When the last one ran off, its head looking oddly large for its body, Emma heaved a huge sigh. "That's that, for this year." She took Jeanie's hand and walked down near the pasture fence. "See, they're fine. They had to get their wool off or they'd be hot in summer."

They watched the lambs hunting for their mothers bleating, "Baa, baa," and the mothers answered with their deep "Baas" until each lamb was matched with its own mother and blissfully nursing.

Emma went along to Merrill when Roy took the wool to the woolen mill and picked out yarn and a quilt bat. Then she and Jeanie went to the dime store while Roy went to the hardware store.

Jeanie stood wide-eyed as she watched the little cans whisk back and forth on cables from the salesgirls to the cashier, high in one corner of the store, while Emma bought needles, bias tape, and some peppermint candy.

They were hardly out of town before Jeanie was sound asleep, cuddled against Emma's plush coat. "Those little eyes took in an awful lot today," Emma said.

It seemed a shame to wake her when they got to Tomahawk but they had to stop at the A&P. Roy carried her in and she perked up when she smelled the freshly ground coffee and heard Emma and Roy chatting with the white-aproned salesgirls. She giggled when they pulled down a box of corn flakes with a long stick with big grippers on it.

Roy carried out the fifty-pound sack of flour on his shoulder and came back for the box of groceries. What kind of candy did they give us?" he asked.

"Chocolate drops."

"Ugh. Too sweet. Carl'll eat 'em."

Emma dug in her purse. "How about a peppermint? I bought some at the dime store?"

Roy reached for one without taking his eyes off the road.

Emma never traveled the stretch of road between home and Tomahawk without thinking of all the trips Papa had made. "Used to take Papa all day," she mused, knowing that Roy was following her thinking. "And here we've gone clear to Merrill and back in a half a day—comfortable as can be, all closed in like this."

Roy is certainly enjoying the car, she thought. He had managed to go out at least one evening a week all winter— even in heavy snow. Emma knew he was involved with the young people in Ogema. Thank goodness he wasn't going to dance halls like he had a few years ago.

She didn't even want to think about what Henny would do once he had a car and could get out on his own.

Did me good to get out, she thought that night as scenes of the day flickered before her mind's eye. *I almost forget there's a big world out there*. She thought of all those fine homes with electric lights and bathrooms and all, and wondered if those people could possibly be as content as she was—kerosene, worn linoleum and all.

One March evening Emma brought out the catalog and waited until Roy turned a page of the paper. Then she slid the catalog across the table to him.

"How do you like this linoleum for the kitchen?"

"Hmmm. Don't think you better plan on it right now."

Emma pulled the catalog back. "Oh, that's all right. If you don't think we can afford it, there's no hurry." She put the catalog back on the shelf.

"No, that's not it," Roy said, frowning and biting his lower lip. "Ma, come sit down. I've got something to tell you." He shook his head and took a deep breath. "Ma, Helen and I are getting married."

"*Married!*" Her hands fell in her lap.

He nodded.

"But I don't even know this—this Helen—what's her name—Risberg, isn't it?"

"But I do. Oh, Ma, she's one special girl." His eyes lit up as he continued. "Never met a girl like her before. She's not just a pretty girl with nothing upstairs. She *thinks*. She's got definite opinions and she reads and learns. You remember when I brought her home last fall one Sunday? Carl and Lou Ella Anderson were with us."

"Hmmm. Real dark hair, brown eyes?"

"Uh-huh."

"Not overly friendly as I remember."

"She's shy, Ma. But not with me. We talk and talk."

"Pretty, that I remember."

He beamed.

94

"But where on earth are you going to live?"

"Well, that's what I want to talk to you about. We were thinking that if we moved your cookstove into the front room . . ."

"My cookstove in the *front room!*" Her voice rose.

Roy held up his hand. "Hold on, now! It's right next to your bedroom and big enough for this table—without the leaves—and a couple of chairs and your rocker and the chair Hank likes and we'll get you a cupboard for your dishes."

Emma shook her head and covered her face with her hands. "No—no. I can't talk about it now."

Roy came around the table and put his hands gently on her shoulders. "I'm sorry, Ma. We'll work something out. But we *are* getting married."

The next day Emma moved in a daze. Everything she saw and used—her beloved east window, her convenient flour bin, all the spacious pantry shelves, the pump right outside the door and her sink, all anchored her to her present way of life.

At bedtime she tried to pray, but all she could get out was, *Father, help me!*

The next day was even worse. She stood in the front room doorway and tried to imagine being shut in that room with windows both darkened by the porch. And no sink drain! "At my age I should start carrying a slop pail again!" she grumbled.

At noon she caught Roy studying her solicitously, but she went about her work as though nothing had changed. It wasn't easy to ignore her throbbing headache, though, especially when Jeanie decided this was the day she wanted to "play" the piano. Over and over Emma distracted her to a quieter activity, but her high-pitched little voice cut through Emma's ears no matter where she was.

When Jeanie was finally down for a nap, Emma heated

the coffee and poured herself a cup, thoughts churning. She hadn't even asked Roy when they planned to get married or anything.

Got to ask him—but I'm not going to let him think I'm all for it!

She finished her coffee and went to water the plants in the bay window. *The bay window!* What on earth would she do with the big carnation she took in each fall and all her geraniums and the Christmas cactus she'd had since she couldn't remember when? And the fuchsia and the Wandering Jew and the huge Boston fern on the pedestal? She began to cry, quietly at first, and then, when she was way back in the pantry, she let the sobs roll out.

Eventually, she fished a hanky out of her apron pocket and mopped her face.

"Got to get hold of myself," she said aloud. "Ain't the end of the world!"

But when Jeanie woke up crying and crabby, Emma felt like crying all over again. "I'm supposed to take care of this child like a young woman, but now I'm supposed to sit in a couple little rooms like an old lady," she sputtered.

That night when she had Jeanie in bed, she picked up her knitting without a word.

Roy cleared his throat several times and finally said, "Forgot to tell you. We set the date for the first of October. Figured that'd be a good time. Fall work'll be done and the weather still nice."

Emma swallowed and nodded. She couldn't answer. Tears were too close.

She did feel a bit relieved the next day knowing six months still remained before the wedding. *A lot of water will run downhill by that time*, she told herself and got through the day a little better. But, by evening, tension had tightened its grip on her and her head ached again. She'd better go to bed before she said something she'd regret.

"I've got a headache," she told Roy after Jeanie was in bed. "I'm going to bed."

"Sleep good, Ma," he said gently.

If only I could talk to Clara, she thought the next day. She didn't want to ask Roy to take her to visit Clara. She didn't want to ask him for anything right now.

Her opportunity came a few days later when Roy offered to drop her off at Clara's on his way to Phillips.

When Max took Jeanie to see the kittens, she said, "Clara, Roy's getting married!" and promptly burst into tears.

Clara sat down, dishtowel in hand. "Why, Emma! Don't you like the girl? Who is she?"

"I don't even know her. Just saw her a couple times. Helen, her name is. Helen Risberg—Herman Risberg's daughter—you know, the carpenter. He died a couple of years ago."

"I don't know them but I've heard they're a nice family."

Emma dried her tears and blew her nose. "It's just," she started to cry again, "that I'm not ready to be shoved off in a corner. I can't give up my house!"

"But where else could they live? You and Jeanie don't need all that room, and Carl and Hank aren't home that much anymore."

"I know, but it ain't fair! I've got this little one to take care of like a young woman; yet I'm being put out to pasture like an old mare! Roy thinks we should make the front room into a sort of living room/kitchen combination 'cause it's next to my bedroom."

"That room's nice and big."

"But my bay window and my sink and my pantry—"

Max came in with Jeanie riding on his shoulders and Emma hastily turned to help Clara set the table so he wouldn't see her red eyes.

"Hey, Auntie!" Max said as he speared a fat slice of home-baked bread. "Roy told me he's getting married in the fall. It'll be kinda nice for you to have a woman to talk with for a change, won't it?"

Emma smiled a weak smile, knowing Clara was shooting him warning looks.

But he went on. "That Helen sure is religious. Can't get Roy to go to dances or even have a beer anymore."

Emma's brows shot up. "So that's why he hasn't been going to dances!"

Clara smiled as if to say, "See, there's one more thing to be thankful for."

"Anyway, there's a few months yet," Emma said as she dried dishes.

"Are you hoping they'll break up?"

"I don't know. Guess I've been thinking so much about myself that I haven't thought about them," she admitted ruefully.

"Maybe when you've seen them together, you'll feel better about the whole thing. Why don't you invite her over?"

"I hadn't even thought about that."

"She sounds like a nice girl. I always wanted to go up the Risberg hill but never had any reason to. Folks say it's a beautiful place up there and the winding road through the woods is so pretty—there's even a lake partway up the hill."

As Emma left, Clara put her hand on her arm and said, "Emma, you care about that boy, don't you?"

98

Of all things to ask her! Of course she cared about her son. She *loved* him—but that wasn't a word she used easily nor lightly.

The next day Emma's indignation boiled over. *Care about him!* Why, Clara should remember how Roy took over when Papa died. She should know how grateful Emma was for his dependability, and Clara surely knew how well they got along. Emma sliced bread and muttered, "Why, there isn't much I wouldn't do for that boy!"

She caught her breath and clapped her hand over her mouth. What had she said? Suddenly she felt light-headed and sat down—thoughts whirling.

O Lord, I've done it again—got so tied up feeling sorry for myself, I couldn't see anything else, she prayed. *Where do I start? Help me, Father! If I really* care. . .

She hurried to her dresser and opened her Bible where a little slip of paper stuck out. "Charity suffereth long, and is kind . . . seeketh not her own . . . is not easily provoked . . . endureth all things . . ."

Forgive me, Father. I've been so selfish. Help me let go of it! I want to love like I'm supposed to. Help me!

Gently, she laid the Bible down, leaned over close to the old spotted mirror and said out loud, "Emma Verlager, you've got a lot of planning to do!"

CHAPTER 12

THE NEXT DAY EMMA HAD a lot of time to think while she ironed. *I'll think about Roy and Helen and get my mind off myself,* she resolved. *It's going to take some doing to feel happy about this change, but at least now I'm willing to try.*

She set the iron back on the stove, detached the handle, and laid it on the gray speckled reservoir cover, while she put more wood in the stove, hung up a freshly-ironed apron, and picked up another iron.

Helen—she tried to recall every detail of the girl. Certainly looked different from her brown-haired, blue-eyed daughters. Not only was Helen's hair dark brown—almost black—but bobbed! Emma couldn't picture Ella or Gertie or Minnie or Mamie or Sadie or any of them with short hair. But then, times change. No reason why they shouldn't cut their hair, too, one of these days instead of wearing it pulled back severely.

She unrolled a bundle of sprinkled pillowcases and began

to iron one Emmie had embroidered for her. Helen would never know Emmie. Would she ever understand how she had been loved? Would she think less of her when she learned of Emmie's hasty wedding? Roy said Helen played piano. It wouldn't be easy to have this dark-haired stranger play Emmie's piano—but she'd get used to it. Helen surely had the hands for it. Except for Mamie's, Emma had never seen more graceful hands—long, tapered fingers and lovely oval nails. She recalled shoving her own in her apron pockets the day she had met Helen, suddenly conscious of her square hands and stubby, short-nailed fingers. She sighed. Roy surely must be thrilled to hold those lovely hands.

She turned the pillowcase over, pressed it hard to make the embroidery stand out. Then she carefully folded it, giving it a quick swipe with the iron after every fold, as the pleasant, fresh-air fragrance floated up around her.

Suddenly she wanted to see Helen again. She wanted to see them together.

That noon, after she had tucked Jeanie in for her nap, Emma stood, arms folded, surveying the front room.

Yes, they'd have to do something about the arch—double doors put in, maybe. There'd still be room for the cookstove on that wall, and space for a bench for the water pail to the left of her bedroom door. The table and chairs would fit to the right of it. She'd push the table against the wall to save space.

She studied the elaborate etched-glass door window—a stag with antlers her sons would prize. Too fancy for a kitchen, but then, that end would be the dining/living room end. She'd keep the wooden rocker right where it was. Henny liked that one. And the square walnut table with the scalloped edge and ball-and-claw feet could stay there in front of the north window.

She measured the remaining wall space with her eye. Her rocker could go by the east window and the rest of the wall could be for a little washstand with mirror and a cupboard. She turned and walked out on the narrow porch with its railing all around it. Uh-huh. The railing at the end could come off.

That evening, right after supper, she beckoned to Roy. She led him through the house and out the front door. "Look here," she said, pointing to the railing at the end of the porch. "How about taking that section off so I can carry my slop pail out this way? I can throw it out back of the lilac bush at the edge of the field."

His surprised expression gave way to sheer delight and she had to blink back tears.

He peered over the end and said, "Pretty high. We better have Floyd build a step—a big wide one."

"I think I'll transplant a honeysuckle back here and make a flower bed along the house. Never did much with this end before," she rambled on, not wanting him to comment on her change of heart.

A little later, as she poured the dishwater down the drain and listened to it gurgle, she thought, *What's an old sink drain compared to that boy's happiness?*

After chores, instead of the usual quick wash-up, Roy mixed shaving lather in his shaving cup and carefully frosted his face. He turned to Emma, brush in hand. "Everyone comin' over for your birthday Sunday?"

" 'Most everybody, I guess. Gert says she's baking my cake."

"Good," he said, twisting his mouth to the left and scraping carefully with his safety razor. "Guess it's time to tell 'em the big news."

"How come you told Max the other day?"

Roy tilted his head toward the light and kept shaving.

102

"Oh, I guess I just hadda tell someone." He frowned. "I asked him not to tell."

"Well, it's high time the family knew or there'll be hurt feelings."

She heard him take the stairs two at a time. When he came down in a crisp shirt and corduroy pants, she asked, "You going to see Helen?"

"Yep!" he said with a grin which mellowed to a gentle smile as he said, "Ma, thanks!" And he was gone.

Sunday, as usual, the men congregated in the dining room; the women, in the kitchen. The dining room, once the spacious kitchen before the addition had been built on, was rarely used for dining. Now it served as an informal living room—a "family room."

Emma watched Ella. Her cheeks looked unusually rosy with excitement.

Emma had some news of her own. She'd had a letter from Ed the day before. She waited for a break in the conversation but, when none came, she broke in loudly, "Girls! We had a letter from Ed yesterday. Connie's going to have another baby in the fall."

There were a variety of exclamations.

"That'll be four already . . ."

"All so close . . ."

"Wonder how Connie's feeling?"

"Ed's a lot of help around the house."

Ella piped up, "I'm going to have a baby, too—in October."

Then there *were* exclamations!

"I thought Gracie would be my last. After all, I'll be thirty-seven."

"Oh, forgoodnesssakes!" Emma exclaimed. "You

103

could have a couple more yet. I was forty-one when Hank was born."

"Oh, Ma! Don't say that! Seven is enough!"

They were laughing and talking so loudly they didn't even hear a car drive in. Emma turned to get the coffeepot and there stood Roy in the doorway—with Helen standing shyly at his side.

"I'd like you to meet Helen Risberg—soon to be Helen Verlager. Helen, you've met my mother and this is my sister, Ella, and sister Gertie, and Mamie, Al's wife, and my sister Minnie—"

Everyone was talking at once.

"Congratulations!"

"When's the wedding?"

"So happy to meet you, Helen."

The men came to see what all the commotion was about. There were more introductions while Emma set more places at the table and urged Helen to sit down. She didn't cling to Roy physically, but her eyes pleaded, "Please don't leave me!" Roy sat down with the women.

They didn't stay long. They had to tell her sister Lily's family, and her brother Nels and his family. Her brother Leonard, and her sister Gayla, already knew.

After the couple had left, all eyes turned to Emma. Ella asked *the* question. "Where are they going to live?"

Emma was able to tell them all about the plans without even once feeling like crying.

That night at bedtime, Emma whispered, "Lord, You are so good! You worked it all out. A week ago I could have just bawled, but now I can talk about the plans like they were my idea in the first place. But Father, when things get rough, please help me remember how those two look at each other."

In May Emma's thoughts went beyond her own little world as she tried to imagine how Charles Lindbergh felt flying over thirty-three hours across the Atlantic Ocean, all by himself. Conversations at mealtimes and before and after church centered almost exclusively around his flight.

One noon, after Emma had read more details in the paper, she said, "My goodness! What would Papa say? Whoever thought anyone would fly across the Atlantic Ocean?"

"Al says there'll be airplanes big enough to carry a hundred people someday," Hank said, cutting a picture of the crowd of nearly one-hundred thousand people greeting Lindbergh at an airport near Paris, to tack-up in his room.

Emma chuckled. "Sounds like Al. Maybe it will happen, but I don't think I'll live to see it."

Lindbergh's flight gave the youngsters a new hero, Emma realized when she saw the little boys—arms outstretched—playing airplane at the Fourth of July picnic.

"Oh, yes," Mamie said, "they both want to be pilots."

Though it kept Emma busy watching Jeanie that day at Pearson's Lake, it was a happy day. Roy brought Helen for a while but then they left to spend some time with her family.

Helen still said very little—just smiled a lot.

"Oh, to be young and in love." Gertie sighed as they drove off with enough space on Helen's right for another passenger.

That summer one scene repeated itself several times.

Emma and Jeanie would be sitting on the porch swing when Roy drove out in his shiny blue Overland with peonies, roses, or whatever happened to be in bloom, nodding in the crystal vases mounted inside the car on the post between the windows. The dialogue was always about the same.

"Where's Roy goin'?" Jeanie would ask.

Emma would answer, "To see Helen."

Jeanie would pout, "Always goin' ta see Helen."

"That's 'cause they're going to get married."

"I wanna get married, too!"

"Not for a year or two, *Liebchen*."

After such a dialogue Emma could see Roy and Helen doing all those young-parent things with Jeanie that Emma's stiffening joints prevented her doing—splashing and running in the lake, coasting on the crust in winter and skating on the pond.

She wanted to share those dreams with Jeanie but she certainly didn't intend to foist the responsibility for Jeanie's care onto the young couple—not as long as she was able to take care of her. *But should there be a time she wasn't able—*

The day before the threshers were due, Roy said, "Well, Ma, next year Helen'll take over. She'll need your help, but you won't have the full responsibility."

And so Emma faced the threshing dinner with a blend of nostalgia and relief. That evening, as she hung up the dishpan, her mood was definitely one of relief. She crept off to bed, bone-weary.

The first day of October dawned clear and quite warm. Once more Emma inspected Roy's and Carl's suits that she had painstakingly pressed the day before. Carl and Lou Ella would be the attendants.

Emma and Jeanie rode to Ogema with Carl in his little Ford coupe—early enough to spend a few minutes at Gertie's before the wedding. Jeanie's dad and his friend, Amanda, were there! He coaxed Jeanie to sit in his lap for a few minutes by showing her the picture of her and the lamb he carried in his wallet.

When they left for the wedding, Ed took Emma's arm and apologized for not visiting for such a long while.

"That's all right," she told him. "You have your own life now." What she really wanted to say was, "We can manage without you."

In church Emma was too preoccupied keeping Jeanie quiet to think sentimental thoughts, but when the organ music began, her throat tightened. She looked up at Roy and Carl and realized they were no longer "boys"—but grown men.

When the organ announced the bride's entrance, necks craned. But Emma couldn't tear her gaze from the tender glow in Roy's blue eyes as he watched his bride come down the aisle.

My! She was beautiful and radiant—aware only of Roy, it seemed. *O Father, keep them always devoted to each other—long after this first love-bloom fades,* Emma prayed.

Though Emma talked and laughed with family and friends at the reception in the church basement, her throat ached, and, when they ran through a shower of rice to Roy's car, she let a little sob escape.

Sunday afternoon when Jeanie was taking her nap and Carl had stretched out on the couch, Emma said, "Keep an ear open for Jeanie, will you? I want to take a little walk."

She cut across the field, over to the stone piles where she and Jeanie had picked spring flowers, up through the pasture, and across another field to the site of the old house.

There was nothing but a rectangle of stones and high weeds now. Too bad they couldn't have somehow preserved it. She tore off some dry grass around the flat stone that had served as the doorstep and sat down. Hugging her knees, she studied the landscape to the north—the house, barn, tool shed and the trees tucked in between the buildings. Then she turned south to the river.

It was twenty-five years since they had left the little house but it seemed like yesterday when she was hanging out clothes, watching Al tear out stumps and plow those first little fields. And they'd stand at twilight looking over the newly cleared section, basking in the elation of accomplishment and Al would tell her his latest plans. He was always the one to plan, while she hung back with more of a let's-wait-and-see attitude. It was when he stopped making plans that she knew he had given up hope of living.

When his pain got worse and worse and the doctor operated only to close him back up, she knew only a miracle would save him. But miracles were scarce in those days.

Suddenly she realized that Helen would never know him. How, she wondered, would this shy girl have coped with his teasing. How she wished he could know all that had gone on. She wanted to tell him, but it wasn't right to try to talk to dead people—was it? *Lord, will you tell him? Tell him how well Roy has done and that Carl is going to be a fine young man and Henny—just tell him he's a real trapper—like my brother Fred. Oh, and tell him—tell him—I miss him.*

A torrent of sobs rolled out into the quiet. They came and came until she wondered if there was an end to them. Then, when they had subsided and she had dried her eyes, she decided to walk up into the woods through the autumn leaves.

Why, she wondered, as she strolled along through the rustling leaves, *doesn't a person notice how black tree limbs are when the leaves are green.* Surely they didn't suddenly turned darker as the leaves turned color. Now they stood in stark contrast to the countless shades of gold and red.

A moss-covered log invited her to sit down. "Father, I don't understand," she spoke aloud, her words quivering in

108

the stillness. "Why do I feel so empty? I want to cry every time I see the way those young folks look at each other. Am I jealous? I guess I am—in a way. Al never did look at me like that. Things were sort of matter-of-fact. Oh, you know, we loved each other. We had a good marriage—but there wasn't that special something I see between these two. Oh, but I'm not yearning for another man! Goodness, no! I've got all I can handle right now! It's just—I guess I'm love-hungry. Lord, I know You love me but I don't *feel* Your love. I do feel love for You. It's been there ever since I was a little girl and my uncle called me 'the little heathen' because I hadn't been baptized. One day in that little church in Oshkosh I told You I didn't want to be 'no heathen'— that I wanted to belong to You all the rest of my life and be with You for all eternity—but then, why do I feel like this?"

Looking up at the black branches, brilliant leaves and blue sky, she started to cry until tears ran down her cheeks and on down ner neck.

"Jesus—Jesus—I feel so empty."

Something was happening. Something that had never happened to her before. She didn't breathe. She didn't move, except to close her eyes. What was it? Something soft, warm, falling over her and through her, permeating every cell of her body. It was like being held with infinite tenderness. "O Jesus," she breathed, "it's You. It's You. Oh, thank You, thank You!"

Tears ran unheeded. "I love You, I trust You."

Oh, if I could stay like this forever, she thought. But that special indescribable something was going, going, gone— leaving a peace she had never experienced before and a new joy glowing deep within her.

"Oh, my!" she said aloud. "I never imagined there could be anything like this. Lord, You're so good to me! I don't deserve it!"

How long had she been here? She had lost all sense of time. She'd better hurry home.

Back through the dry leaves she rustled, through the fence and, scarcely glancing at the old house site, hurried toward home—each step a thank-you.

What had happened? She didn't know, but one thing she knew: that empty feeling was completely gone!

During the next week she kept up the regular work and tried not to be too curious about the various crates that stood in the tool shed. She did investigate the ivory-and-blue stove, running her hand over the shiny enamel of the warming oven. Who ever would have dreamed of a colored stove? She peeked at a corner of the roll of linoleum—blue, to match the stove—as well as the green one for her room—the one that she had looked at for so long.

She went out, shaking her head. *Did these young folks appreciate all these new things?* She and Al had been content with homemade and hand-me-downs. But why shouldn't young people have pretty new things if they could afford it?

The week dragged and the boys were unusually quiet. One night at suppertime she said, "You'd think we've just had a funeral around here, not a wedding." And Henny had said, "Sure is going to be different around here." And Carl had said, "Won't ever be the same."

She hadn't even thought that the boys would be affected by the change.

The morning after Helen and Roy came home, Emma's heart lurched when she saw Roy's car in the yard. He didn't get up for chores. Emma tried to keep Jeanie quiet, but around eight, she gave up and let her "play" the piano.

Jeanie stopped abruptly when the stair door opened. Roy and Helen stood in the doorway, hand-in-hand. Jeanie dashed to Roy and he tossed her up in the air.

110

Emma watched, laughing. When she looked at Helen her laughter ended. Helen was watching, too. But she wasn't smiling.

CHAPTER 13

THE DAY ROY AND HELEN CAME HOME, things began to hum. Carl had decided to stay and work with Roy in the woods for a few months and Hank hadn't started trapping yet, so the three of them worked together laying the linoleum in the front room, moving Emma's stove in and helping Floyd, the neighborhood carpenter, install the double doors and build the porch step.

Helen's kitchen floor was laid next and the bright blue-and-ivory stove set up. Meanwhile, Helen painted a drop-leaf table and four chairs blue and ivory to match the stove. She even painted a little bottle to use for a vase. "I'd never have thought of doing that," Emma told her.

It wasn't an easy week for Jeanie. She had an exceptional talent for being right where someone wanted to move.

One morning she played a long while with the new door knobs—glass, with a star design deep inside. "Mama, look! Ain't they's butiful?"

"She calls me 'Mama,'" Emma explained to Helen, "but she knows I'm her grandmother, not her mother. The pictures of her parents have helped me explain things to her.'' The oval portraits of Emmie and Ed were left where she had first hung them—one on each side of the north front-room window.

Sunday came fast that week. As Emma dressed for church she wondered how many people were curious about Roy's bride. Not all of them had been at the wedding.

Emma took her usual seat on the women's side, expecting Helen to follow her. But Helen followed Roy to the *men's* side! They must have agreed she would sit there, because Emma didn't think Roy looked a bit perturbed.

Not daring to look around to see the reactions, Emma stared at her toes as her cheeks grew warm. *That's all right! About time we broke that tradition, she thought,* remembering when Fred was home how she had wanted to sit with her boys. But she was quite certain that the incident would be the table topic in many homes that noon.

''Helen, I'm glad you sat with Roy. Seems a woman should always be by her husband's side—especially in the house of God.'' Helen smiled politely, and Emma realized she didn't feel the need to be sanctioned by Emma or anyone else. She had strong convictions and acted on them.

Once the furniture was moved Emma set about completing the details of her compact home. The once-elegant, ecru, tatting-edged curtains Gertie had made years ago now hung limp and dreary. Emma hung fluffy-dotted white Priscillas in their place.

The little glass-doored cupboard Roy had bought posed another problem. It had been designed to display attractive pieces, not Emma's hodgepodge of dishes and groceries. White gathered curtains, hung on the inside of the doors, hid its modest contents.

One evening, after Jeanie was tucked in, Emma sat down with a sigh. So far she certainly hadn't felt useless or

113

shoved into a corner—not with Carl and Hank still to cook and wash for. In fact, she wished she weren't quite so busy so she could go and help Ella a little after their babies came.

If only she were closer to Connie with her four little ones. Baby Mary Lou had joined the family on September third. Connie certainly had her hands full.

Tuesday, October, 14 Roy poked his head in the door and said, "Hank just called. Ella had a baby boy!"

The next day he took Emma over to see little James Alton. Ella was doing well, but Emma sensed that Jeanie's clamoring to see the baby and hold him was making Ella nervous, and Mrs. Summers seemed to have things well in hand, so they didn't stay long.

"How are things working out with you and Helen?" Gertie asked Sunday, when they had stopped by after visiting Ella.

"Fine! Just fine!" Emma could answer honestly. "She says there's no reason why my plants can't stay in the bay window. I don't think she's fond of that big fern, though. She says I can keep washing on Mondays 'cause she knows I always like to get the washing out of the way the first of the week. We'll both use the sewing machine. I can move it in here when I want to. It really is nice to have a woman to talk with. Sometimes we talk for a whole hour."

"I'm glad. It isn't easy for two women to live under the same roof. They both have to be generous."

Later, when Emma was alone, she thought, *Helen* is *generous—with everything but Roy.*

When Jeanie had run into Helen's kitchen after supper and promptly crawled up on Roy's lap, Helen had ushered her back into Emma's room and shut the door firmly behind her.

Little Jeanie hadn't understood, but Emma had. It wasn't

easy, she knew, to have an old lady and a little child always around when you're a newlywed.

She's young, Emma said to herself. *Right now her heart can't hold more than Roy. But it will grow—in time.*

In November one of Hank's dreams came true when he found a young hound for sale. He named him Sport. "He's a small hound," Hank assured Emma. "He won't eat much."

Emma, relieved that Henny wouldn't be alone way out there in the woods, patted his sleek head. "Seems like a nice dog. We'll feed him by my door and hope he doesn't bother Colonel."

Christmas was the liveliest in years with Helen and Roy's guests coming and going. This time Jeanie turned completely around before she spoke her recitation.

Al had made her a little doll crib, and Emma had made tiny sheets and a puffy comforter. She was delighted when she saw it under the tree.

Ed had sent two little dresses, but he didn't come to see her. "Just as well," Emma said when Jeanie couldn't hear her.

But the nicest part of Christmas was Helen's playing Christmas carols on the piano.

New Year's Eve, 1928, found Emma alone again but she didn't mind at all. There were even more family members to pray for this year—

Lots of changes she hadn't even dreamed last New Year's Eve had already been completed. They hadn't been easy but she was content. Still, she was never free of concern for Jeanie. So many more years to go before she'd be on her own.

During a Sunday-afternoon visit with Nels and Minnie, Minnie blurted, "Ma, we're moving to California."

"You're *what?*"

Minnie nodded—close to tears. "Nels has been reading about it and he thinks he can get work. It does sound wonderful, Ma. We'll have an auction and sell everything we can't take. We'll buy a tent and a camp stove and Nels will build storage spaces in the Model T. Oh, Ma, it will be fun! Amy is ten. She's a lot of help and Johnny is four. He isn't a baby any more."

"I know—but the desert—the heat—and not even a closed car."

"That's why we plan to leave in May, just as soon as school is out."

Emma tried to smile. "I've got to get used to the idea, I guess. But when will we ever see you?"

"I can't think about that. You know Nels. When he makes up his mind—"

"Well, you let me know how I can help you."

It hadn't been easy to hold the tears back that day, but Emma had tried to be cheerful. Now, in bed, she felt tears slide down her cheeks and into her pillow.

Lord, I can't bear to think of not seeing them for years.

Minnie sent a picture postcard every now and then as they headed west, but Emma yearned for the day when she would get one with an address on it. Three weeks on the road and they still weren't at their destination.

"Think I have a bad case of spring fever," Emma told Helen one May morning. "I don't want to stay inside. Want to come out and see where the perennials are?"

Helen dried her hands, slipped on a sweater, and followed Emma. They made a tour of the yard and decided that Helen would have the east side of the house and front yard. Emma, the west—except for the "stone jar," as the planter

116

made of field stone and mortar was called, where she always planted her red carnation.

Emma raked leaves away from the sprouting iris, bleeding heart, peonies, and tiger lilies while Jeanie romped with Colonel. Tomorrow she'd work on the west side of the house and plant a little honeysuckle and dig a new flower bed.

Could it be possible that a year ago she had been so upset about Roy's getting married? Now that her life had settled down, she was glad she didn't have the care of the whole house. It was enough to take care of her two rooms and Carl's and Hank's bedrooms.

One of these years, when Carl got married, she'd fix his room for Jeanie. But she wouldn't think about that for a long time.

It was June before Minnie sent their new address. Emma promptly wrote back to tell her that George and Sadie had a new little girl named Betty.

Several weeks later Hank told her he'd be going with Carl out to Devil's Lake, North Dakota, to work in the harvest fields.

"That should be good for him," she told Roy. "He needs to get out in the world a little. Maybe he'll think of something besides trapping and the woods."

With only Jeanie and herself to wash and cook for, Emma had time to go visiting a little more. She loved to go over and help Ella and hold little Jimmy. He was a cute little fellow but, she told Helen, "I'm afraid he is going to be one spoiled child. The older children cater to him something awful."

By July the paper was full of Al Smith and Herbert Hoover.

"Who are you going to vote for, Ma?" Ella asked one day as Emma shelled peas.

117

"Well, it won't be Al Smith. I was reading that he's against prohibition."

"But things haven't gone too well with all the bootlegging and bathtub gin and everything. People are getting poisoned!"

"Humph!" Emma interrupted. "Serves 'em right for drinking the stuff. Like I always say—"

"Oh, Ma, don't start! I know you hate drinking. Do you really think Hoover can put 'a chicken in every pot and a car in every garage' like he's promising?"

Emma laughed. "Don't know as I've ever seen a politician's promises kept. But who knows? Time someone got in there and did something for farmers once instead of only bankers and businessmen."

In September Carl and Hank came back from North Dakota. Carl stayed only long enough for Emma to do his laundry before he took off for Muskegon. Didn't seem like he was going to be home much anymore.

In November Emma was among the happy ones when Herbert Hoover was elected president. "Now we'll see who'll have chickens in the pot," she said to Ella.

Day after day, that November, Emma waited for a letter from Carl. He had written that he had a job at Continental Motors and then, a few weeks later, that he had been laid-off and was in Hart doing odd jobs for room and board.

The next time she wrote, she enclosed a stamped envelope. Maybe that would bring an answer.

It did. He wanted to come home but didn't have the twenty dollars it would cost. Would she send it?

Twenty dollars was in the mail the next day.

The evening Carl came home, Emma let Jeanie stay up past her bedtime and she sat on Carl's lap while he told about his experiences.

118

"When I went to put in my application at Continental Motors they told me I had to go to a high-school principal and get a work permit because I wasn't twenty-one. Well, they gave me a form to fill out and, along with a lot of other stuff, they wanted the names and ages of my brothers and sisters. I was sittin' right by the secretary and she was watching me. Well, I started with Al. I knew he was forty-one. I sure didn't know all the other ages so I just put each one down two years younger than the last one. But when I had about seven of 'em down, I heard the secretary snicker and I could feel my ears gettin' red. I kept writin' but before I got to Roy I had all the spaces filled up and she laughed right out loud. The principal came and looked and said, 'Quite a family you have there.' But he was real nice and gave me my permit and I got out of there fast."

It was good to have Carl home.

Fortunately, Carl got a job in August Johnson's camp and Hank started trapping so that winter Emma again hung out wool socks, long underwear, flannel shirts, and overalls which froze almost before she got them on the line—as did her fingers. But it was worth it to have her boys home weekends.

CHAPTER 14

A TRIP! A real honest-to-goodness stay-overnight-on-the-way trip! It had sounded wonderful when Gertie had asked Emma to come along with them to visit Fred and Helen in Muskegon, but still she protested: "It will cost so much money!"

"But Ma, we're going anyway. It won't cost anymore for you and Jeanie to ride along." She sat down at the table with Emma, eyes shining. "Oh, it will be fun! We'll go around the lake on the way there and coming back we'll cross on the ferry. And Fred says wait'll we see their beach—snow-white sand! Won't the kids have fun?"

"That's another thing—the three of them riding all that way—"

Gertie dismissed that problem with a wave of her hand. "Did you ever see two kids play better together than Earl and Jeanie? And Clyde is so quiet—thank goodness! Oh, I wish it were June instead of April!"

Emma ordered dress material, pulled the sewing machine in her room, and sewed a dress for Jeanie and one for herself.

"Does Jeanie have a bathing suit?" Helen asked one day in May.

"Oh, forgoodnesssakes, I never thought of that. No. She doesn't."

"I've got an idea," Helen said and went upstairs.

She came back with a red-and-blue stocking cap, one long enough to hang way down the back. "We could make her one from this. Cut the neck and holes for her arms and legs, and crochet around them."

"Why, I'd never have thought of that! Of course! I'd hate to have to buy one."

While Emma sewed dresses, Helen worked on the bathing suit.

One day Gertie called and said, "Joe says you should stay overnight here the night before we leave. I know the train always wakes you, so we'll just get the kids up and leave at five."

"I feel like a little kid, counting days," Emma told Helen. "I think I've mentally packed that suitcase half a dozen times already."

The afternoon before they were to leave, Roy took them to Gertie's and carried in her straw suitcase—the one Papa had bought when he was on the town board and had to stay overnight in Phillips.

"Have a good trip, Ma," Roy said, "We'll take good care of your chickens and you greet Fred and Helen for me."

That evening Jeanie perched on Gertie's kitchen stool while Joe cut her hair straight-around, even with the bottom of her ears.

"Who are we going to see on our trip?" Gertie asked her, smoothing her shiny bangs.

"Uncle Fred and Aunt Helen and Kermit and Everett," she answered, waving her arms and kicking her feet all the while she talked.

121

"And that's supposed to sit still for two days in the car?" Emma said behind her hand.

The lonesome whistle of a train—was she at Gertie's? Emma opened her eyes and saw pink rosebud wallpaper and soft light flowing in around the edges of the window shade. The tourist room!

Now she remembered and joy flooded in. Today they'd see Fred, Helen and the little boys! She wanted to jump right up and get going, but there wasn't a sound in the house and Jeanie was asleep beside her.

Oh Father, You're so good! Thank-You, thank-You for this trip. Thank-You for this soft bed and the good sleep. Lord, help me be patient and loving—all that You want me to be today and keep us safe as we travel.

Jeanie stirred, opened her eyes and said, "Mama? Where are we?"

"We're in a tourist room, remember?" Emma whispered.

She yawned and sat up. "What's a 'tourist'?"

"Someone who travels. *We* are tourists."

"Are we *always* gonna be tourists?"

Emma chuckled. "No. Only while we're on our trip. Say! Do you know what's going to happen today?"

Jeanie sprang up and started bouncing on the bed. "We're gonna go to Uncle Fred's house!"

"Shh! And don't jump on the bed! Come on! Let's get dressed. I hear Earl and Clyde."

They were ready when Gertie knocked on the door.

As they stood outside waiting for Joe to tie the luggage on the top of the car, Emma looked up at the big white house they had slept in. "Don't you wonder why people with such a fine house like this take in tourists?"

"Oh, Ma, didn't you see the man sitting in the wheelchair way back in the house when we came in last night?"

"No. I didn't. I was watching Jeanie so she wouldn't touch anything."

A cloud of sadness drifted over Emma's joy as they drove away. "Lord, bless them," she whispered.

Fred had just gotten home from work when they pulled up in front of the little gray-shingled house with the rose trellis in front.

"Ma! You don't look a day older!" Fred exclaimed as he hugged her. "A bit grayer, though."

"And fatter! Never have been this heavy! You look good, Fred."

While the grown-ups exchanged greetings, the four boys eyed each other and then ran off to see the rabbits, Jeanie right behind them.

"She looks like Emmie," Fred said.

"Doesn't act like her, though," Emma said. "She talks, talks, talks—just like her dad."

Fred laughed. "As I remember, Emmie always had plenty to say."

"I suppose. But Jeanie's different."

After supper, as they sat around the table, Emma said, "Isn't it wonderful how those years melt away once we're together again? Doesn't seem like it can be five years since we've seen each other."

Emma could hardly believe her eyes when they went to the beach. The sand *was* white. The children played at the edge of the water while the grown-ups visited in the shade.

That afternoon Fred sat down near Emma on the front porch. "Haven't had a chance to talk to you. How are things going for you?"

"Fine! Roy's wife and I get along real well. Oh, we do things differently, but we put up with each other."

"And Jeanie?"

"The hardest part is always wondering if I'm doing the right things—it's a different kind of responsibility than I had with you kids. Makes such a difference being older." She sighed, "If only I can live till she's through school."

Quickly Fred changed the subject. "Al wrote that business has been bad at the blacksmith shop and he's thinking about coming to work here. Has he said anything to you?"

"Not lately, but I know he doesn't have much business."

"Well, tell him things look pretty good here right now."

The morning they left, standing on the ferry deck, Gertie took a deep breath and said, "This is how the ocean must be. Can't see a bit of land."

"I want to look and look so hard that I'll never forget all this blue," Emma said. "Just think, Gert, when we get home and we're ironing or washing dishes, we'll still see this in our mind's eye."

Gertie laughed. "Aren't you glad you came?"

They couldn't find tourist rooms in a private home that night, so they went to a hotel. Emma had never seen so much glass and silver as in that dining room. She spread the huge white napkin on Jeanie's lap and prayed she wouldn't spill her milk.

What luxury! A bathroom for every room! Jeanie reveled in the big white tub, until Emma said, "Look at your feet! They're wrinkled as a prune," and she lifted her out, protesting, and wrapped her in a fluffy white towel.

The closer they got to home, the more eager Emma became. She hadn't been away from home this long since Hank was a baby—eighteen years ago. She and Al had gone to Oshkosh and to Wind Lake to see their birthplaces, but she had gotten so homesick they had come home sooner than planned.

"I just don't know how to thank you," she told Joe when he carried in her suitcase.

Jeanie grabbed his hand. "'By, Daddy-Joe," she said softly. She had called him "Daddy-Joe" the whole trip.

He gave her a hug and went off chuckling.

"It's good to go, but it's good to be home again," Emma told Roy and Helen.

August 19 Len called. "We have a *boy!*"

"Oh, I'm so glad," Emma exclaimed. "How is Nora?"

"Fine!"

"What did you name him?"

"Leonard! Leonard Junior. What else?"

"We went to see Len Junior today," Emma told Ella on the phone three weeks later. "Dimple in his chin just like his dad. Think he might have the Verlager ears, too. Oh, I was so embarrassed! Jeanie ran in with Joy Ann and, by the time I got in there, Jeanie was *washing the bathroom!* Her straw hat was still hanging down her back and there she was washing the sink, walls, floor—everything—with a nice white washcloth. And you know what a good housekeeper Nora is!"

Ella laughed. "I can just see her. I suppose all those smooth surfaces felt nice. What did Nora say?"

"Oh, she laughed and laughed. Wouldn't let me get after her—we stood and watched for a few minutes. She said she'd remind her in about twenty years and see if she still liked cleaning bathrooms that well!"

When Gertie came for a Sunday visit, she said, "Guess what? I'm going to board the schoolteacher. She seems like a friendly young lady. Her name's Olga Harrold. Tiny little girl."

"That will be nice for you. Joe is gone so much you'll have someone to talk with. I remember how I enjoyed having Jenny Clark with us when Papa was working in the woods. I'd knit or mend and she'd read to me."

125

Gertie laughed. "Well, I don't know if Miss Harrold will read to me, but I'm looking forward to having her with us."

In September Ed wrote that they had another little boy, Richard. He promised that *next* summer they would be sure to get home.

By September it was evident that Helen and Roy were going to be parents sometime in the winter. Helen hadn't said a word about it, and Emma didn't ask. Usually women talked to each other about their expected babies, but Helen didn't.

Emma had given Al Fred's message about available work, so she shouldn't have been surprised when Al and Mamie came and told her that he would leave for Muskegon before school started. Mamie and the children would stay with Mamie's folks until Al got settled.

"I guess it wouldn't seem so far away if we hadn't just driven there," Emma told Gertie.

Nevertheless, she was determined not to make leaving any harder for Al than it was. But that determination hadn't come lightly. She had gone to her "patterns" seeking the right attitude. The Bible didn't mention the virtuous woman in Proverbs ever having to cope with her family members moving away, but she did find guidance in the other pattern: 1 Corinthians 13. There she saw that the loving thing to do was not to concentrate on her own sense of loss but to be patient, kind, and to *hope*. She would not think, *I won't see them for years,* but, *They* will *come to visit or I'll go there. Maybe they'll even move back again.*

The determination, however, was only the first step, she discovered. Her feelings didn't necessarily agree. The day after Al and Mamie's auction, as scenes of the torn-up household set her heart aching. She talked it out with the

126

Lord—told Him she knew that His will was that she be concerned for them, not herself, but that her emotions didn't agree one bit! *You're going to have to help me, Lord. I'm counting on You to give me Your peace so I can think about them and not myself.*

"I thought you'd be much more upset about Al leaving," Ella told Emma one day as they cut string beans for canning.

In the midst of interruptions Emma managed to tell Ella about her decision and how the Lord had helped her.

Sadie's little boy born October 22 was named George. "This must be the year for Juniors," Emma said.

The next week Emma complained to Helen, "'Stock market crash; stock market crash!' That's all that's in the papers these days. I don't understand what it's all about."

"I don't know a lot about it either," said Helen. "Evidently many people thought life wasn't worth living when they lost their money, because today's paper said many were jumping out of windows."

"Oh, my goodness! Guess we can't understand what it would be like to lose everything."

"Money isn't everything," Helen protested.

Emma agreed. "It certainly isn't. But a lot of people haven't learned that yet."

CHAPTER 15

FOUR DAYS AFTER CHRISTMAS, Jeanie woke up with a rash on her forehead and her chest. *Measles.*

"How did I ever take care of all those sick children through the years?" Emma asked herself. Now she was exhausted taking care of one little measly-girl.

By January 4, Jeanie's rash had faded and her fever was down, but Emma tried to keep her quiet and warm.

"This is it!" Roy told her when she went to the separator room to get milk that morning. "I've called Doc, and Leonard is bringing Helen's mother over."

"How's she doing?"

Roy shrugged. "Good. She says she doesn't have pain—just knows something's going on."

"I've heard of women like that," Emma said with a rueful laugh. *But I never knew any,* she thought.

It was late afternoon when Roy came downstairs, saying, "It's a boy! We named him 'Ronald Risberg'."

Later, after the doctor assured them that the baby was naturally immune to measles, Mrs. Risberg brought the baby for Emma and Jeanie to see, Emma kept Jeanie a good distance from him anyway, explaining, "He'll be here all the time. You'll be able to see him every day."

"Ma," Roy said, coughing as he talked, "will you let the girls know? I don't feel so good."

She felt his brow. "My land, boy! You're burning up! Have you had the measles?"

"Not that I remember."

"Good thing you have that hired man. Let him do the chores tonight. You stay here with Jeanie and me."

That night Emma had Lloyd bring down a mattress for Roy to sleep on. He didn't get up for chores the next morning.

Three days later he started breaking out with measles. In another day the fever went down a little.

Mrs. Risberg took full charge of Helen and the baby while Emma kept the heater stove roaring, took care of Roy, and tried to keep Jeanie quiet.

Dr. McKinnon insisted that Helen stay in bed ten days but she could sit up on the eighth day. Emma made brief visits but was still afraid she'd carry germs.

When Carl and Hank came home from camp that weekend, Carl offered to stay home.

"Naw, I'll be up in a couple days," Roy said. "Lloyd can handle the chores till then."

But by Tuesday, instead of feeling better, Roy had chills and fever.

"This isn't right," Emma said, as she tucked the comforter around his shaking shoulders. "You were starting to feel better and the rash is gone. We'd better have the doctor check you."

Roy was too sick to protest.

Dr. McKinnon thumped and listened. Frowning, he said to Emma, "Pneumonia. Right lung's really bad. Keep him warm. Give him lots of liquids and I'll leave some medicine to help him cough up that stuff.''

Pneumonia.

The dreaded word echoed in Emma's ears. Nothing doctors could do but hope the patient's body was strong enough to fight it. Emmie's hadn't been. First the childbed fever, then pneumonia. But Roy was strong. He had been healthy—up to the time he took measles.

Her hand shook as she poured coffee for the doctor.

Mrs. Risberg read fear in her eyes when Emma told her what the doctor had said.

''He'll be all right,'' she said assuringly, ''but Helen had better stay upstairs another day or two.''

Got to think of more I can do, Emma told herself. First of all, she could pray. And pray she did—fervently.

So cold! Must fight cold air. Keep Roy protected. Each time someone opened the kitchen door, frigid air swept through the house. Emma cringed, imagining it attacking Roy through every thin spot in the covers and blowing icy shafts down around his neck.

She lined chairs along the foot of his mattress and draped blankets over them. Whenever she walked past, she hunted for gaps she might have missed, and if she found some, pinned them shut.

At noon she had Lloyd bring in a bucket of oats, filled ten-pound sugar sacks with them, and heated them in the oven. These she tucked along Roy's back and chest as he rested on his side. Every hour or so, she'd replace them with warm ones.

One time she'd find him chilled; another, drenched with perspiration. She'd help him strip off a soggy flannel nightshirt and don a dry one. She tore pieces of soft rags for Roy to use for handkerchieves and set a bag beside him to put them in. When it was full, she burned it.

130

The wash rig wasn't ever put away those days. It stood in the corner of Helen's kitchen. When Mrs. Risberg wasn't washing for Helen and the baby, Emma was doing the rest of the laundry. The drying rack behind the stove was never empty.

During the day distractions kept fear at the fringes of her thoughts and, usually, she slept soundly from sheer exhaustion for the first part of the night. Every hour, though, she'd wake up as though she had a built-in alarm clock—fix the fires, change the grain bags and do what she could for Roy. Immediately, she'd go back to sleep for another hour. At about four o'clock, brain alert, body still exhausted, she'd wage the thought-battle.

She was a doe chased to the point of collapse by a pack of wolves where she lay surrounded by fear-thoughts intent on destroying her.

Pneumonia—lungs filling, filling, shutting off breath and life—You know he's getting worse. Lungs filling, filling—You thought Papa couldn't die. But he did. You thought Emmie couldn't die. But she did. You think Roy can't die. But—no! No! Lord, help me! The fires. The grain bags!

Back in bed she'd whisper, "Thou wilt keep him in perfect peace, whose mind is stayed on thee; because he trusteth in Thee."

Father, I trust You. You promised that all things work together for good to them that love You. You know I love You, and another hour of sleep was hers.

From night to night the fear-thoughts and subsequent words of comfort varied, but not the pattern—until several nights after the doctor had been there. Toward morning, the thoughts began to plague her again and she felt anger boil up within her. "In the name of Jesus," she spat out, "leave me alone!"

The thoughts fled and she slept.

131

Thursday morning Helen came down, smiling but pale, her mother and the baby right behind her. Roy propped himself up on his elbow to see the baby, but when he began to cough, Helen took the baby into the kitchen.

Emma didn't blame her for wanting to come downstairs, but she was concerned about having them close to Roy.

Helen wasn't afraid. She had Lloyd bring a narrow cot down from upstairs and that's where she nursed the baby and slept at night. The baby slept in a clothes basket she had painted ivory.

Roy still had terrible spells of coughing and alternately burned and perspired, but he seemed more alert. Small wonder, with Helen and the baby right there to motivate him.

The day after Helen came downstairs her brother Leonard came and got his mother. ''They'll be fine,'' Emma assured Mrs. Risberg when she left.

She was weary. The washing, cooking, fire-tending, nursing she could handle. It was trying to keep Jeanie quiet that exasperated her. The child needed to run and jump— but where? How?

She looked out of the window and saw Lloyd piling wood. She nodded and smiled. That noon she asked him if Jeanie could ''help'' him and winked over Jeanie's head.

He said he certainly could use some help, so out she went in her brown coat and leggings, and helped him pile wood.

''Bless that boy,'' Emma whispered as she shut the door behind them.

''I'm going to take a little nap while Jeanie's out,'' she told Roy and Helen.

Oh, that bed felt good! ''Jesus,'' she whispered, ''You said all that were weary and heavy-laden should come to You for rest. I come to You now. Rest my body. Restore me. Keep me strong.''

When she heard Jeanie on the porch she got up, smoothed her hair, slipped on her glasses, and set her face smiling.

The next day Lloyd took Jeanie to the barn to help him feed the cattle at noon.

"Father, you are answering my prayer for help and I thank You," she whispered, and off she went to bed.

But when Lloyd came in for supper on Friday evening, he was coughing the same dry cough Roy had had.

"Oh, no!" Emma groaned. "Let me feel your forehead."

"I'm all right," he insisted.

"No, you aren't! You have a fever. Have you had measles?"

He shrugged. "I don't know."

Emma shook her finger at him. "You're going right up to bed. We can't have you down with pneumonia, too."

"But the milking?"

"I can do it. There aren't that many cows milking now," she said as she tied on her *kopftuch*.

Colonel barked. A car drove in.

Emma opened the door. "Carl! Are we glad to see you!" she called out.

Carl had quit his job. He started a whole string of reasons why, but Emma didn't hear. She was busy thanking the Lord.

Emma felt sorry for Lloyd alone upstairs and tried to go up often during the day.

Roy gradually got better. "Praise God, Praise God," Emma whispered as she worked, but she kept an eagle eye on Roy. If he went out too soon he'd have a relapse.

She knew Roy hated to tell Lloyd that he wouldn't need him any longer now that Carl was home, but Lloyd had presumed he wouldn't, and had asked Carl to take him home as soon as he was feeling better.

133

Things became calmer. The highlight of Jeanie's day was when Helen bathed the baby. She wanted to bathe her dolls, too, but Emma explained that cloth or composition dolls could not be put in water. To make her happier, Helen powdered them. She was delighted because they smelled "just like baby Ronnie—when he doesn't need to be changed."

One day in February, as Emma watched Roy stride across the yard with an armful of wood, gratitude welled up inside her again and she whispered, "Father, thank-You. You are so good!"

Hank came home from camp and helped Roy with chores. Carl took a job driving trucks, staying at a tiny hotel in Ogema.

"We've been seeing a lot of Carl lately," Gertie told Emma a few weeks after he took that job. "He comes over several nights a week."

"That's nice," Emma said. "He must get lonesome for the family."

Gertie laughed. "Well, Ma, I don't think that's quite the reason. Looks to me like cupid's at work."

"You mean Carl and Miss Harrold?"

"It's a little soon to tell, but I'm hoping it's really serious. You've met her. You know what a special little gal she is."

Emma decided she hadn't better tell anyone—yet—but she was delighted. *Where on earth would they live, though?* Carl didn't have any savings or even a steady job and Gertie said much of Olga's money went to her mother, who was rearing several children alone.

Oh, well, they'll find a way. Young lovers have a way of doing that.

Gertie said one day in April, "Ma, I just had to call you

134

and tell you the latest romance news. Last night Joe had to meet the train at Spencer and he asked Carl to drive him over. I had a notion that Carl wanted to ask Olga to go along, so I ducked in the pantry. I could see them through the crack in the door. She was sitting at the table doing some schoolwork and Carl stood there, shuffling his feet and jingling the change in his pocket, and said, 'Ah—I'm taking Joe to catch the train at Spencer 'n I was—a—wondering—you wanna go along for the exercise?' "

Emma laughed. "Oh, dear, I can just see him."

"She went! I think she really likes him, Ma. When he told her he's going to go to work for Len next week, she looked real disappointed. Won't see him night after night like she does now."

In May Ed wrote that they were coming home in June. "Can't wait to see them," Emma told Ella. "Imagine little Connie with five children. Wonder if she'll look a lot older?"

"I can't imagine Ed with five children," Ella said. "But I bet he's a good father."

Nels and Minnie came back from California in June, too. Nels had gotten a mechanic job at Kiger's Garage. They rented a house about a mile east of Ogema.

They missed seeing Mamie and the children by two weeks. They had gone to join Al in Muskegon.

Ed and Connie's car had barely rolled to a stop before Allison was up in the haymow, Shirley right behind him. Maybelle, a bit more quiet, and chubby little Mary Lou peeked out from behind Ed, and little Dickie clung to Connie.

Ed hugged Emma so tight it hurt. "Oh, Ma, it's good to see you!"

"Connie! You still look like a little schoolgirl!" Emma exclaimed.

Connie laughed. "I can tell you I don't feel like one!"

What a commotion! Jeanie was soon running and chasing right with the rest of the children.

"Such a little cutie, Grandma," Connie said as she watched her. "Looks like the little girl in the Jello advertisement. You have to come and visit us! Look how much fun she's having with the kids."

Every day they visited one of the families. Some days Emma stayed home to catch up a bit. Jeanie refused to go without her.

"I'm worried," Emma told Connie. "She starts school this fall, and she doesn't want to go anywhere without me."

"Oh, she'll be all right when she sees the other kids."

Emma sighed. "I hope so."

Emma told Connie how often she had wished they lived closer so she could help her.

Connie smiled. "I wish you were closer, too, but I want you to know you can be so proud of your son! He comes home from the mail route about three and pitches right in and helps me."

Emma could see that. Every evening, when they came home from visiting somewhere, Connie would nurse the baby and Ed would bathe the others and get them ready for bed—laughing, singing, teasing all the while as Connie watched adoringly.

"Does your heart good to see them," Emma told Minnie. "The way they look at each other—and they enjoy those little ones so much. I won't be so concerned now after seeing them. Such a happy little family."

One day in August Helen hung up the phone and said,

136

"That was Ruth Anderson, the new school teacher. She needs a place to board and wondered if we'd be interested."

"Hmmm. Ruth's a quiet, pleasant young lady. She'd be nice to have around—and the money would come in handy. I guess she could have the room at the top of the stairs if she wouldn't mind leaving her door ajar for heat."

Ruth came over and said the room would be fine. Helen and Emma papered it with blue-flowered paper and Helen put down new woven rugs and hung white ruffled curtains. Ruth would be surprised when she saw it again.

Before school started, Emma went along to Tomahawk and bought Jeanie a little red pencil box and a lunchbox with Red Riding Hood on it. She added a can of salmon and a loaf of bakery rye bread to the grocery list. (Jeanie always picked salmon sandwiches with rye bread when the ladies had their meetings.)

That first day of school Jeanie ate little breakfast and promptly lost it. *The first day of school is bound to be hard for her*, Emma thought.

Emma took her, near tears, into the classroom. When the older girls rushed over and gathered her in, Emma quickly left.

That night Jeanie talked and talked and Emma sighed a deep sigh. She *liked* school!

But the following morning, up came her breakfast again.

Emma walked to the fence line with her but when she turned to go home, Jeanie ran back and clung to her. Arvid Johnson saved the day when he stopped and asked if she'd like a ride. Reluctantly, she climbed in beside Donald, who was a year older.

Again, the next morning she threw up what little she had eaten and didn't want to go. Emma walked with her until she could see the school. Jeanie went the rest of the way alone, crying.

"I just don't know what to do," Emma told Ella. "I feel sorry for her but she has to go to school."

"Does she say why she doesn't want to go?"

"No. She just cries when I ask her. And she's such a skinny little thing, I can't stand to see her lose her breakfast every morning."

Miss Anderson said Jeanie was fine once she got to school, and seemed to be a bright little girl.

All through September, October, and November, Jeanie had an upset stomach every morning and begged to stay home. Emma packed extra lunch for her and she did eat something at morning recess and kept it down.

One snowy day when Henry came to pick up Jeanie on the logging sleigh for school, she refused to get on the sleigh. Henry got down, picked her up, and put her on it, but she jumped off and ran to the house.

Emma waved them on, helped Jeanie take off her coat and overshoes, and told her to get in the big bed. Then she pulled her straw suitcase from under the bed. She took one of Jeanie's dresses off the hanger, folded it, and put it in, saying, "Well, if you won't go to school here, I'll have to send you to your dad."

"No, Mama! No, Mama!" she screamed. "I'll go! I'll go!"

Emma held her close and they both cried. She hung up the dress and put the suitcase back under the bed.

"I feel awful!" Emma told Ella. "She's probably scared of her dad 'cause she doesn't know him. You know how long it's been since he's been here and now that he's married again, who knows if he'll ever come. But I had to do *something!*"

The next morning Jeanie lost her breakfast but she went to school without a fuss.

The excitement of the upcoming Christmas program kept

138

her going each day and Emma hoped she'd be better when school started after Christmas, too. If she wasn't, she'd have to take her to the doctor.

CHAPTER 16

"I DON'T UNDERSTAND IT," Miss Anderson told Emma when school resumed after the first of the year. "Jeanie enjoys school and she gets along well with the other children."

"Well," Emma said with a sigh, "I was hoping she'd be better but now I have no choice. We're going to take her to the doctor."

Dr. McKinnon poked and prodded and pointed his little light in Jeanie's eyes, ears, and mouth. "Nothing wrong, except she has a nervous stomach. She'll outgrow it. Give her cod-liver oil in the evening to build her up a little."

Emma thanked him as she helped Jeanie with her coat. "I'm glad there's nothing seriously wrong. It's so different from raising my own. I'm just too old. But if I can just live till she's through school—"

Dr. McKinnon's eyebrows shot up. "Jeanie, go wait with Uncle Roy. Grandma will be right out."

He took Emma's arm and ushered her back into his examining room, out of Jeanie's earshot.

140

"Sit down, Mrs. Verlager," he said. "Do you remember the last words you spoke a few minutes ago?"

"I think I said I hoped I'd live till Jeanie was through school."

"You did." He reached over and took her hand. "Now, if you were a little girl and you heard your grandma say that—"

Emma's lip trembled. "Ohmygoodness! You mean she's scared?"

He nodded. "Maybe she doesn't actually think it out, but way down, she feels that if she doesn't *go* to school, she won't ever get *through* school and you won't die. Understand?"

"I think so. I never realized—"

"I know you didn't," he said gently. "I don't think it will do any good to try to explain it to her. Just don't *ever* say those words again!"

Emma's legs trembled as she got in the car.

That night, after Jeanie was in bed, she talked it over with Roy, Helen, and Miss Anderson. They agreed that it was possibly the reason for Jeanie's fear.

"I have an idea," Miss Anderson said. "I'll ask Jeanie to walk with me in the morning to 'help me' before school. I'm only there half an hour or so before the first children come."

The next morning they held their breath as Miss Anderson suggested it to Jeanie. She didn't have time to get nervous that morning and away she trotted beside Miss Anderson, feeling important.

"You will never know how grateful I am," Emma told Miss Anderson two weeks later.

In January Ed wrote that he and Connie were expecting another baby about the end of February. Emma stuck the letter back in the envelope with a sigh. *Was this the way my*

141

mother had felt each time I announced that another one of our thirteen was on the way? Oh, well, she consoled herself, *they certainly are managing well and are all healthy and happy. They'll manage one more.*

"How's the romance coming along?" Emma asked Gertie, when she, Joe, and the boys came for dinner.

Joe chuckled and Gertie shook her head. "Joe isn't helping it any. Oh, how he teases that poor girl! Last week he pulled a dirty trick. She waited for a letter day after day and none came. On Friday she picked up an ad, and there were three letters stuck inside. I was wondering, too, why Carl hadn't written. He usually writes several times a week."

Emma tried not to smile as she said, "Why, Joe! Shame on you!"

Joe shrugged and feigned innocence.

Ed and Connie's announcement came the last week in February. Little Eddie had been born the twenty-first.

Emma tried to imagine little Ronnie with a new brother or sister. Dickie was only three months older. Though Ronnie was walking well and saying a few words, he still seemed like a baby.

The first week in March Ed phoned. Connie was in the hospital in Durand with childbed fever.

Emma was glad Helen and Roy weren't home just then. She sank, weak-kneed, into the nearest chair. "Oh no! Not little Connie!" She could see her as she was last summer— short brown hair bouncing as she walked, smooth young arms holding the baby and MaryLou clinging to her skirt.

"O Lord, no! Don't let her die! There must be something doctors can do. This can't be your will that these young mothers die," she sobbed. Not once, that she remembered, had a woman ever survived childbed fever.

She called the girls and they tried to sound hopeful but fear crept into their voices.

142

That night Emma slept little and prayed much. *Father, Jesus said that whatever we asked of You in His name— believing—You'd give it to us. I pray for Connie's recovery, but I can't believe she'll be all right because it has never happened before that I know of, but Your Word says 'with God nothing is impossible.' I want to believe that.*

The next night was a little better. During the day she kept busy and was distracted from fearful thoughts, but at night fear smothered her once more.

Ed wrote hopeful letters and Emma clung to those words until March twenty-first: "Mama, can you come? I need you."

Emma told Miss Anderson she was taking Jeanie out of school and the next day Roy drove them to Eau Galle.

They stopped in Durand at the hospital. Ed tried to be cheerful in front of Connie, lying pale and hollow-eyed on the high bed.

She smiled at Jeanie. "Hello, little Jello girl. Come give Auntie a kiss."

Jeanie shrank back.

"That's all right," Connie said. "I don't look very kissable, do I?"

At night, the children in bed, Emma fought thought-battles and prayed, *Father, I ask You, for the sake of all the husbands and all the children who could be left, to help someone discover a medicine for childbed fever. I know You don't want these mothers to be taken from their families.*

During the day Jeanie played happily with the children but at bedtime she often cried. The children knew more than the adults had realized. One night she said, "I don't want Aunt Connie to die! Why can't God make her well like He did in the Bible? I don't like God!"

Emma lifted the sullen little chin with her finger and said, "No, *Liebchen*, don't be angry at God. God is a loving

143

God. Maybe we just don't know what He wants us to do. In the Bible, He has all the instructions for how we are to live. Maybe we just haven't found them all yet."

Jeanie reached up and hugged Emma and said, "I don't wanna be mad at God."

"Neither do I, *Liebchen*, neither do I."

The third day, Emma and Jeanie stood at the doorway where Connie struggled to breathe, openmouthed. "Sometimes she knows me," Ed said. "Want to see if she knows you?"

Emma shook her head and Ed led her, sobbing, down the corridor. Jeanie trailed behind.

When they got home that day, Ed said, "I won't come home again now until—" and he hurried out to the car.

Emma heard the children talking the next day. Little Maybelle said, "Poor Mama. Poor Mama." and Shirley said, "What do you mean, 'poor Mama'? She'll be in heaven. Poor *us!* Who's going to take care of us when Daddy's on the mail route?"

The morning of the twenty-eighth Ed came home. "Mama's gone to be with Jesus," he told the children. The girls cried, but Allison set his little jaw and blinked hard.

By evening the first carload of brothers and sisters arrived. More came the next day.

Emma longed to find time and a place to cry and cry but there was too much to be done. All these little ones . . .

Connie, dressed in a lovely rose-colored dress, was laid out at her parents' home. They took the older children to see her. Again, the girls cried. Allison didn't.

Emma couldn't stop trembling the day of the funeral. She barely heard what the minister said. She was relieved when she heard Allison say to Ed, "Daddy, hold me tight!" And he cried and cried.

Out of church, into cars, past the house, out of the cars—

144

Emma stared at the flowers piled high. *Will we be able to see them from Ed's kitchen window?* she wondered. Why did that cemetery have to be so close?

The next morning, when they were ready to leave, Ed picked up little Dickie and came outside to see them off. The other four clustered around him. The baby was asleep in the house.

Ella and Emma struggled to keep smiling until they were out of the driveway but they were miles away before they dried their eyes.

Later that day someone mentioned the date. Emma gasped. They had almost forgotten Jeanie's seventh birthday. They stopped and got ice cream cones to celebrate.

When they got home they learned it was another little girl's birthday. George and Sadie had a new baby Banetta.

But even April sunshine and the new life couldn't burn away the grief-cloud that hung over Emma.

"If only I were closer, I could help Ed," she said to Gertie one day. Helen had insisted she go along to visit Gertie while Roy took care of some business in town.

"Ma, you want to help all of us. But you're only one person. Come, sit down and have a cup of tea. I've got something to tell you—two things!"

"Well," Emma said, teacup in hand, "what's the big news?"

Gertie leaned close, although there was no one else in the house. "This is a secret. I heard Carl and Olga talking the other day. They're planning on getting married in June!"

"I'm glad! Goodness knows they don't have any money—but they'll manage somehow."

"They're just going off over a weekend by themselves, I think."

"Ohh—I'd like to see them get married!"

Gertie sighed. "I would, too, but they said no matter

145

how small and simple they made it, it would be too costly. And with this family, there's no way to keep it small.''

"What's the second thing?'' asked Emma, after they had savored the news about Carl and Olga.

Gertie giggled and hugged her middle. "I'm so excited! I'm going to have a baby in August!''

Emma set her cup down with a clatter. "You are! Why, I never suspected!''

"Maybe I'll get my little girl yet!''

"Gertie's having a baby in August,'' she told Roy later.

"Good!'' he said. "Bet she's hoping for a girl.''

How can young people be so glib? Emma thought. *We've just seen Connie lying there—I should have more faith. I should be the one they can lean on—and here I am with this knot of fear inside of me.*

The next few days she was impatient with Jeanie to the point of exasperation, irritated with Helen, and abrupt with Ronnie when he came for a horsy ride on her foot.

Her throat and head ached, and no matter what she ate, her stomach felt queasy.

The third day—the warmest of the season, so far—she put on a sweater and overshoes and tied on her *Kopftuch* and, sweater clutched around her, she walked down the hillside out of the wind and leaned against an elm tree.

A tiny smile tugged at the corners of her mouth as she realized where she was standing—right where the old outhouse had stood. This towering elm had been a mere twig beside the door at first. But by the time they moved to the new house, it was a good-sized tree.

Its rough bark bit into her back but she didn't mind. It was solid, unmovable, something to lean on.

"Ohforgoodnesssakes, such a silly thought,'' she muttered. "Leaning on a tree when I should be leaning on God.''

146

But He was way up there someplace—far above that blue spot between the clouds—not here where she could feel His comforting presence.

"Why are you so far away? I need you," she whimpered. Immediately a thought took shape in her mind and she spoke it out, "He can't be in the same place as fear. My fear has shut Him out!

"Oh, Lord, I'm so ashamed! I'm so scared! All I can see is Gertie lying there, like Emmie, like Connie, and Joe standing there with three little ones. I can't get rid of it myself. Help me let go of it. Father, I want to trust You. Give me something to cling to."

She waited, expectantly, but all she could hear was the boisterous river and the wind high in the branches of the budding trees.

More desolate than when she had come, she started for home. Foolish to expect the answer so quickly and on the spot. Yet she kept hoping.

She wandered along the fence that curved with the contour of the river. At the beginning of the next curve Papa had buried the stillborn baby. She leaned on the fence, eyes searching through the brush. Yes! There they were. She could see the thorny branches of the Wind Lake roses she had planted almost thirty years ago—after she had recovered. She had been so sick. "We didn't think you'd live," Mrs. Geber had told her later.

She walked on, feeling the spongy wet sod beneath her feet and the sweet spring wind on her face. "I'm *here!*" she said aloud I could have died. Papa could have been standing there alone with the ten young ones. *O, Lord, I don't understand why I'm here and all those other young mothers had to leave their families. All I know is that I trust You. I can't live with fear. I want to let it go. I can take anything as long as You are with me. Jesus, I love You.*

She hurried toward home. Must be getting late. Jeanie would be home soon.

She wasn't aware until she was coming up the hillside behind the barn that the horrid old knot of fear was gone.

CHAPTER 17

EMMA PRETENDED TO BE surprised when Carl told her about their wedding plans. "You certainly have my blessing," she assured him.

He told her they would be married in Glenwood City, Olga's birthplace, and that they would be living over Len's garage.

Emma wasn't happy to hear they had ordered furniture on time payment but she had to agree they had no choice. "I never yearned to be rich," she said, "but at times like these I certainly wish I could help."

Carl laughed. "Oh, we have to have a few hard-times stories to tell our kids someday. Don't worry about us. We'll be fine."

When Emma told Jeanie about their marriage, her eyes opened wide. "Miss Harrold will be my aunt? Oh, boy!" She wanted to know where they were going to live and when they could go to see them.

She didn't have to wait long. A week after they got back Nora had a reception for the newlyweds and the whole family was invited.

Mrs. Evans, Nora's mother, baked one of her special angel food cakes and circled it with fresh bridal wreath. Jeanie's eyes sparkled as she whispered, "Oh Mama! I never saw a cake with flowers around it before. Isn't it pretty?"

Gertie found a seat next to Emma. "Oh, don't they look happy?"

"Looks like she'll fit right in," Emma said as Olga laughed and talked. "I'm so glad we could all get together like this."

Ella sat down near them. "Did you hear? They were married at high noon, June 6. The minister's wife and hired girl were witnesses."

Gertie laughed. "Can't you hear it some day when their daughter wants a fancy wedding! They'll tell her about their wedding and remind her that big weddings don't guarantee happy marriages."

In July Connie's Ed came home for a week and brought the children and his hired girl, Evelyn.

"Oh, dear," Emma confided in Ella. "She's such a giddy young thing. You don't think Ed—"

Ella laughed. "Oh, Ma. Ed has more sense than that. She's just a hired girl. He can't manage all six children alone."

A few weeks after Ed went back home he wrote that Evelyn had run away with a neighbor boy one night. He had found a lady who could stay a few weeks, but he asked for prayers for more permanent help.

When Emma had read the latest letter from Mamie, she took it to Helen and went back to her room without a word.

Helen usually stood in the doorway and talked but today she sat down. "I can't imagine what it's like to live in the city and be out of work," she said.

Emma sighed. "They don't even have gardens to depend on. Sounds like both Al and Fred were laid-off at the same time, doesn't it"

Helen nodded. "She did say they expect it to be temporary."

Emma pounded the arm of her rocker with her fist. "Right away, when something like this happens, my mind starts going lickety-split—trying to think of some way to help, or of something they can do to help themselves. It's worry. Plain old worry, that's what it is." Emma clasped her hands together and shook them for emphasis. "Got to stop worrying. It's all right to be concerned but I've *got* to put them in the Lord's care—pray His power into their lives, not try to do something myself."

Helen nodded. Words weren't necessary, but Emma knew she agreed.

The first weekend in August Emma and Jeanie stayed overnight with Carl and Olga. Jeanie thought it odd to live upstairs, but she liked running up and down the stairs and she admired their new furniture—especially the ivory-and-green stove and green wicker rocker.

One day, during their visit, a knock on the door sounded, and there stood Jeanie's dad. The more Ed apologized for not visiting, the more uncomfortable Emma felt. Jeanie was at least polite, though she stayed close to Emma.

"She looks so much like Emmie," Ed said, trying to control his emotions.

Red-eyed, but smiling, Ed asked Jeanie if she'd write to him.

She said she would.

"I'll write back," he promised.

He pulled out his wallet, handed her a dollar bill, and said, "You go and get a treat before you leave town."

"Would have been better if he hadn't come," she told Olga later that evening. "Only upsets her. He has another family now."

"Got a letter from Mamie today," Emma told Ella in August. "They're coming home! They want to be back so the children can start school. They'll stay with Mamie's folks until they can get their own place again."

"That's good. But what about Fred. Did he find work?"

"Nothing steady, but they've lived there so long he has a better chance of getting odd jobs than Al. When that letter came I started thinking and worrying about how they'd get started here again. Why do I always have to get myself all riled up before I have sense enough to go to the Lord?"

"Oh, Ma, after all, it's just human nature to worry."

"That's no excuse! We have the Spirit of God in us to take over and give us power so we can live the way God wants us to."

"But Paul said the things he wants to do, he doesn't do and the things he doesn't want to do, he does."

"You go get your Bible and read that next chapter! We don't have to live that way. I get mad at myself because I don't catch myself right away. Worry is an awful sin. It's saying, 'God, I don't trust you. I think I can figure out a way to solve this problem.'"

"But everybody worries . . ."

"That doesn't make it right!" Emma snapped but continued in a more gentle tone. "Ella, you'll see. Once you decide to let go of worry, He'll set your mind at ease."

"I know you're right . . ."

"You try it then!"

When Emma hung up the phone she prayed for Ella and then went back to work singing, "Oh what peace we often forfeit, Oh what needless pain we bear. All because we do not carry everything to God in prayer."

When Carl and Olga took Emma and Jeanie home the next day they stopped at Gertie's house. Jeanie couldn't understand why "that lady" was in the kitchen cooking while Aunt Gertie sat in the living room and visited. Emma didn't tell her about the expected baby. She told her Aunt Gertie had hired the lady to help her.

August 13 Joe called. It was a boy. They had named him Donald.

Emma was so eager to see Gertie that Roy drove her to Ogema the next day. She didn't have to ask, "Were you disappointed?"

As soon as they came in, Gertie said, "You know how much I wanted a girl. Well, I couldn't find my voice when they told me it was a boy. But once I saw him, I wouldn't trade him for a million girls. Isn't he cute for a new baby?"

"You were that small once," Emma reminded Jeanie. How glad she was that Jeanie was seven! *Eleven more years—*

As the first day of school approached, Emma talked brightly about how good it would be to see all the children again and about all the new things Jeanie would learn.

But the first morning she lost her breakfast. Emma assured her it was only first-day-of-school nervousness—that she'd be fine the next day.

Each morning after Jeanie had left Emma sat on her bed and prayed that the Lord would take Jeanie's fear away. And He did. Then Emma thanked God for bringing Jeanie through that difficult time.

"Lord, You are so wise. You are so good not to let us see ahead. I wouldn't have the courage to go on if I could see all the problems coming up these next eleven years."

That November, though Emma dreaded hunting season,

she was grateful for the opportunity the men had to put away meat for the winter. The men, though they loved the sport of it, hunted in earnest this year.

The deer were hung in the woodshed and the men would bring in a quarter at a time for the women to cut into roasts and to grind the scrappy parts into hamburger with a hand-cranked meat grinder.

What would we do without venison? Emma wondered. The tiny cream check barely covered the cost of flour and oatmeal these days.

One day early in December, Carl and Olga came home. As Emma watched them from the window she knew something was wrong. Usually they bantered and laughed when they got out of the car. Today they weren't even smiling and Carl had his arm protectively around Olga.

"I should have known it was coming," Carl said, eyes on the floor. "I knew Len was barely making ends meet. Guess he held out as long as he could. So many people out of work. Hardly anyone buying cars and most of the time they can't pay for repairs. It sure was tough for him to tell me he had to let me go."

That night Roy, Helen, Carl and Olga stayed up late talking.

The next morning when Carl sat down to the table he said, "Ma, is it all right if we use my room upstairs? Roy's willing to have me work with him in the woods this winter."

"Of course it's all right," she interrupted.

"We're hoping by spring we can build a little log house on the forty I own."

"I don't even know where it is. You boys have bought land here and there. . . ."

"It's next to Hank and Ella's land but a quarter of a mile in from the road. There's an old tote road into it, though."

Emma took a sip of coffee before she answered. "It won't be easy starting out like that," she said, but the mere mention of a log house set her pioneer spirit soaring.

"At least our furniture is paid for," Carl told Emma a week later when the last of it was stored in the tool shed. "We'll have something to put in our house when it's built."

Christmas gifts were simple that year. Ronnie loved it when they all ate together and the table would be full. "Round—round—round," he'd say, making jerky circles with his spoon.

As Olga and Emma washed dishes, Emma said, "You know, this has been the happiest Christmas we've had for a long while. I forget we're poor."

Olga laughed. "Oh, Grandma, so do I!"

"Ah, yes," Emma sighed, as she stretched out in bed that night. "Love will soften the hardships they have ahead of them."

CHAPTER 18

If there's one thing I'll remember about this winter, Emma thought as she undressed one night, *it will be those two planning that house.* She peeked through the crack in the bedroom door and watched them a moment, heads together, as Carl worked with a stubby yellow pencil and an old brown ruler, and Olga asked endless questions.

Doors, windows, roofing, nails, two-by-fours, chimney brick—so many things they'd need. Where would they get the money?

One evening, as they sat working on their plans, Carl said, "Ma, come here. Take a look at this." He slid the paper under the lamplight and pointed with the pencil, "It'll be sixteen by twenty-four with the bedroom back here. Think eight feet is wide enough? Want to save all the space possible for the main room."

"Well—if you turn the bed this way—"

"I was thinking of putting it at an angle," Olga said.

"And here," Carl tapped with the pencil," will be the chimney. And this north window will be the kitchen window."

"Oh, double windows on the south side! That will be nice and light. And the east window in the bedroom—I can just see morning-glories peeking in the window."

"We don't plan to do anything with the inside walls yet—just put in a ceiling and a partition."

"And linoleum, at least on the kitchen side," Olga added. "And, of course, we don't have to paint the windows right away."

"Close as I can figure," Carl continued, "the door, windows, nails, tar paper for roofing, wallboard, brick, and mortar shouldn't run more than a hundred and a quarter."

"Does that include the linoleum?"

"Who needs linoleum?" Carl teased.

"You're going to have to sell an awful lot of wood," Emma said. "You won't get paid for your pulpwood till summer, will you?"

"Nope. Gotta get the money somehow."

A few days later Carl and Roy rattled off to Tomahawk in the old truck, loaded with firewood. They didn't get home until six-thirty.

Olga's eyes sparkled when she saw the empty truck. "You sold the wood!"

Carl concentrated on washing his hands. "Yeah, well, the lady that said she wanted it had already bought some, so we went over to the boardinghouse and the landlady took it. Had it almost unloaded—piled it for her, too—and she yelled out, 'That's fine, boys! You stop by next week and I'll pay you.'" He groaned. "Couldn't even buy flour. Just got kerosene and oatmeal."

Olga bit her lip.

Emma opened the big blue can that held the flour.

"There's plenty till next week and I think Helen has enough, too."

"It wasn't such a bad day," Carl said as he sat down at the table. "Got two orders for next week."

The next day as she peeled potatoes, Olga said, "Grandma, did you have a chimney in your log house or just the stovepipe?"

"The first summer we only had the stovepipe, but then Al built a chimney."

"Can't we put in the chimney later?" Olga asked Carl. "And we don't really need the ceiling or the partition right away, either, do we?"

"Or the linoleum?"

"Well—"

He hugged her. "You don't want to part with that yet!"

"How much would it cost without all that?"

Carl scribbled a few minutes. "Maybe we could get by for about sixty bucks."

The next week, when they came home from hauling wood, Carl shook his head. "The lady at the boardinghouse still couldn't pay. One lady who ordered some wood said her son had brought her a load. We talked the other one into taking it all, but we had to let it go for a buck and a half a cord."

"Did she pay you?" Olga asked, holding her breath till he answered.

Carl nodded. "Hadda buy flour and gas. Ain't much left."

Olga turned to the stove and stirred the stew Emma had just finished stirring.

Olga was her usual cheerful self the following week, but Emma often saw her staring out the window.

Meanwhile, Roy and Carl got up at five each morning, did chores, ate breakfast, grabbed their lunches, harnessed the horses and took off for the woods back of Carl's property to cut spruce for pulpwood that would be sold to the paper mill, and dead tamarack for firewood. As they worked, Carl selected tamarack logs for the house.

When Emma tucked Jeanie in bed one evening, she said in a pensive little voice, "I wish I had lotsa money."

Emma sat down on the edge of the bed. "Now just what would you do with 'lotsa money'?"

"I'd give it to Carl and Olga for their house."

"That's just how I feel. I don't mind having them here—and I know you don't, either—but they should have their own home."

"But where are they gonna get the money?"

"I don't know, but I know who does!"

Jeanie giggled. "I know who—God, huh?"

"Want to ask Him for it?"

Jeanie squeezed her eyes shut and folded her hands. "Father God, if you want Carl and Olga to have a house all by themselves, you gotta help 'em get some more money. They need a whole lot more. Please show 'em where to get it. Amen."

"Goodnight, *Liebchen*. They'll get it. You'll see!"

By the middle of February Emma didn't have to light the lamp until almost six. "So good to see the days getting longer," she said.

"Is it ever!" Olga agreed, smiling broadly.

What, Emma wondered, *is making her especially happy today?* She hadn't stared out the window once.

After supper dishes were done Carl leaned back, fingers laced across his chest, and said, "Ma, we've found a way we could get the money."

Emma dropped her knitting in her lap.

"We could surrender Olga's life insurance policy."

"Oh dear, I hate to see you do that but—"

159

"I've only had it a few years," Olga explained. "It doesn't have much value—about fifty dollars, we think. But we need it so badly."

Emma nodded. "I know. I do have a peaceful feeling about it. I think you should go ahead and turn it in."

The next day Olga wrote the letter and the waiting began.

A few days later a letter came from Ed. "Well for goodnesssakes," Emma exclaimed. "He's getting married! Listen to this." She glanced up to be sure she had Carl and Olga's attention.

Dear Mother and all,

I know this will be a surprise, but I have news for you. I'm getting married in a couple weeks. Her name is Peggy. Her husband died several years ago and she's had an awful time trying to manage with four little ones. I've known her since we've been in Eau Galle and always admired her and I guess she feels the same about me. She's a jolly little person, hard-working, and I've never heard her complain. You'll like her.

Her oldest daughter, Rosemary, is two years older than Allison. Gordon is a little younger than Shirley, and then come Frank and Kathleen. It's not going to be easy to put these two families together, but it can't be any harder than it was trying to take care of them alone. We admit that we aren't madly in love with each other like we were with our first spouses, but we're certainly attracted to each other and we're excited about this new challenge.

We ask for your prayers and your blessing.

Love to all, Ed

Carl shook his head. "Whew! Ten kids!"

By midwinter, with many of the cows standing dry, income was at an all-time low. The long fingers of the De-

160

pression had reached out to the most remote parts of the country.

But, when Emma saw the pictures of the soup lines in the cities, her heart ached and she felt wealthy by comparison. They had a home, wood for heat, venison in the woodshed, eggs from the chickens, vegetables in the cellar, and always enough milk. It was only when her stockings could be darned no longer and Jeanie outgrew her overshoes that she felt the need for money.

The stocking problem was easy to solve. She simply cut off the feet and sewed the end shut. A few wrinkles at the heels didn't bother her. The overshoe problem was a bit more complicated. She knitted heavy socks for Jeanie to wear inside the overshoes and had her carry her shoes to school in a bag.

The thing Emma missed most was coffee. The barley "coffee" she roasted in the oven with a little molasses was barely tolerable.

It was the end of March when Carl said, "Well, we got all the logs hauled out for the house—even a few for a barn. We beat that spring thaw."

"Now, if only the money would come," Olga said with a sigh.

The day before Easter Emma came back from the separator room with pitcher of milk. "The men didn't buy any Easter-egg dye," she told Olga. "They bought some jellybeans and a few chocolate-covered marshmallow eggs, but none of the larger candy eggs. Onion skins make a yellow dye. Why don't I boil the eggs with onion skins? At least they won't be white."

"And tonight we'll decorate them with crayons," Olga added.

Jeanie was delighted with the hand-decorated eggs in Emma's little brown basket.

161

At Easter services, Helen was not the only woman on the men's side. Olga sat with Carl, too.

No new Easter bonnets this year. Probably not a new item of clothing in the whole congregation, unless it was a pair of badly-needed shoes. *Why,* Emma thought, *couldn't the church be this full every Sunday?*

"Jesus imparted His righteousness to us," the pastor proclaimed. "When we come to the Father in prayer He doesn't see us in our sinfulness. He sees us covered in Jesus' robe of righteousness."

Emma closed her eyes. Yes! She could see that glowing robe covering her, making her acceptable to the Father. Oh, she'd remember that when she felt unworthy to come to the Father in prayer.

Jeanie's legs were swinging, swinging. Emma laid her hand on Jeanie's knees.

They were quiet a moment.

"All because of His glorious resurrection—"

Now Jeanie was trying to touch the pew ahead of them with her toes.

"Sit still!" Emma whispered. *Little ones never used to bother me like this,* she thought.

The organ began playing "I Know That My Redeemer Lives" and they sang heartily. Emma smiled down at Jeanie, singing at the top of her high little voice. Full volume now—windows trembling. A thrill of joy flowed through Emma, but it wasn't because of the music. It was knowing *He is alive! Soon we'll be with Him forever and ever!*

The day after Easter Olga came in from the mailbox, waving a long envelope. "Finally!" she said, breathlessly. She fished out the check. "Fifty-eight dollars and sixty-five cents! Oh, Grandma, I can't wait till Carl gets home!"

A building bee was arranged for Saturday. "No women

162

or kids," Carl ordered. "You'd just be in the way. Pack us lunches and we'll make our own coffee over a fire outside."

It was late when Carl and Roy got home. "Even got the roofing on," Carl said. "I've got a lot of chinking to do yet, but it's actually up. Henry and Roy hewed the logs smooth on the inside as we laid each row. That's almost a lost art. Aren't many left who know how to use a broadax. Al did some too—he's real good at it—but he was busy helping me with details, and of course Floyd helped a lot. I never coulda done it alone."

"Oh, I don't know about that," Olga said, "but of course it would have taken a lot longer."

"Gotta lay the floor and plaster the cracks on the outside."

"When can we move in?"

Carl shrugged. "Depends on the weather and what Roy and I have to do around here this week."

Carl worked long hours that week. Friday night he said, "I was thinking—if you women wanna come and see the house tomorrow—"

Jeanie's squealing drowned out the rest of his remark.

Saturday morning Olga baked a pie shell, filled it with chocolate pudding, and covered it with whipped cream. Carrying a chocolate pie all that way wasn't going to be easy, Emma thought, but she knew it was Carl's favorite and Olga wanted to make it a special day.

"When we gonna get there?" Jeanie asked each time they rounded another curve in the old tote road and the house still wasn't in view.

Olga laughed. "I think they took the path of least resistance when they made this road."

"That they did," Emma agreed. "They knew it would only be used to tote supplies to camp, so they weren't about to cut big trees or move boulders."

163

"And here we are, using it for a real road."

"Doesn't it look big? We'll have lots of room," Olga said as they picked their way in and around the tools that were lying about just as the men had left them.

"I like the smell of new wood," Emma said. "Oh, look at those south windows! You tell me what house plants you'd like, and I'll start some for you, Olga."

They ate lunch sitting on the floor boards with their feet dangling down in the crawl space below. Only a few more boards and the floor would be done.

"Hope these boards don't shrink," Carl said. "If they aren't dry enough, we'll sure have cracks between the boards."

Olga laughed. "That way, I could sweep the dirt through the cracks. Wouldn't have to use a dustpan."

The chocolate pie filling had run a bit, but it tasted fine. "Yummy," Jeanie said. Carl ate the last piece out of the pan.

"Mama!" Jeanie called from the east end of the house. "Look here!"

Emma strolled the length of the house. "Looks like an old woodchuck hole to me," she said.

Jeanie giggled and Emma followed her eyes to the bedroom window and through to the silhouette of Carl and Olga embracing in the doorway.

Jeanie drew up her shoulders, hand over her mouth.

"What's so funny? One of these days you'll be in love! Then you'll really understand!"

"Oh, Mama! I will not!" Jeanie insisted.

In early May, the rusty old truck chugged out the driveway, loaded with Carl and Olga's furniture.

Emma caught herself turning to tell Olga something a

dozen times, and at supper time Jeanie poked at her food and said, "I wish they coulda stayed here."

"Oh, it's nice and cozy," Emma exclaimed, the day Carl took her and Jeanie to see the new house. "and the new wood smells so fresh and clean. My goodness! All the color!"

The color. That was the difference, she realized, as her eyes roved from the green-checked tablecloth to the cream-and-green stove, and, to her right, to the green wicker rocker, the multicolored rag rug in front of it, the shiny walnut table with the silver candy dish in the middle—a wedding gift from Nels and Minnie—and all around, through the windows, fast-greening grass and bushes. Her own first log home had been dull by comparison.

No wonder we women like house plants, rag rugs, and patchwork quilts. Everything else was black or gray or brown. We only had tiny windows, so we couldn't even see much of the outdoor color.

"Dinner's almost ready," Olga said as she drained potatoes. "Jeanie, wash your hands and you can put the silverware around."

Jeanie poured a dipper of water into the white enameled washbasin on a shelf next to the stove and Emma added a splash of hot water from the teakettle.

Olga lifted the lid of the ice compartment of the little brown icebox and took out a loaf of bread. "See my bread box?"

Emma peered into its towel-lined depths. "Why, that's a good idea."

"And down here," Olga continued as she opened the icebox door, "I have room for spices, jelly, syrup, and things." Gertie says she has some green-and-white-checked gingham I can have to make curtains," she said when she saw Emma looking at the array of china and cookware on the shelves to the right of the door." Carl's going to make shelves over there for books and things," she said, pointing to the corner to the left of the door, "and by fall we'll have the bedroom partition and the ceiling in."

Jeanie bounced on her toes. "Oh, it's just like playing house!"

Olga smiled. "Well . . . almost."

After dinner they went to see the little log barn Carl was building for the cow and heifer Roy had given him.

Jeanie ran to the little outhouse and, when she came out, she asked, "How come there's only one hole?"

Emma chuckled. "We had a two-holer because there were fifteen of us using it when all the children were home. It'll take a few years before they need a two-holer!"

Carl was showing Emma where he planned to grub in potatoes around some stumps, and she was telling him how well potatoes grow in new ground, when they heard a car coming and saw it bumping along through the brush.

"Oh, forgoodnesssakes! It's George and Sadie!" Emma said.

The whole family piled out of the little black Ford. The older children dragged out a big box and set it down in front of Olga.

"It's your housewarming present," Dorothy said. The older children grinned and the little ones giggled.

Cautiously, Olga lifted the flap. *Cluck, cluck, cluck,* they heard, and out popped a brown chicken's head.

"Oh! A chicken!" Jeanie squealed.

"A cluck!" Glen informed her.

George lifted the cluck out and Dorothy and Norma took out eleven chicks.

"Oh, they're beautiful!" Olga exclaimed, as the hen

166

waddled off down the path with her eleven little ones peeping along behind her. "Thank-you so much!"

"Well, Sadie said self-consciously, "we know Carl loves eggs."

And Olga thanked them again and said, "Come see the house."

The next day Emma told Minnie, "You should have seen all those beaming little faces. They were so happy to be able to give something."

CHAPTER 19

SHORTLY AFTER CARL AND OLGA MOVED, Hank announced he would be staying home for the summer to pitch for the Rib Lake baseball team. At first Emma was happy for him. But later, when she remembered that all the games were played on Sunday and that the team was sponsored primarily by tavern owners, she was concerned that he would be led far from God, and she told him so.

His response was a disgusted snort. "Oh, Ma! That's ridiculous!" he had snapped and punctuated the remark with a slammed door.

Emma saw her prayer-work laid out for her.

By July the lawn was brown except for the shady spots under the box elder trees. When Emma washed clothes, she carried every bit of rinse water to the tomato plants and the few petunias that still bloomed bravely. The hoped-for raspberries thrived only around brush piles and in partial shade, but Carl and Olga were able to pick enough to sell a few quarts.

The following week Emma and Jeanie helped pick, too, and went along to Tomahawk to sell the berries. At the crest of every hill, Carl shifted into neutral and coasted until the car nearly stopped while they guessed, using trees and posts as markers, how far the car would go before he had to put it in gear again. "Someday, when we don't have to be so careful about using gas," he said over his shoulder to Emma, "I'll probably still coast down every hill, I've gotten so used to it."

At the A&P store Emma carefully counted her money. It would be nice to have a box of corn flakes or some soda crackers, but she decided she'd rather spend the twenty cents on ice cream cones for the four of them.

They made the cones last almost to Spirit Falls.

That night, after Jeanie was in bed, Emma had a long talk with the Lord. *Father, I wish I could earn some money— sell something like the woman in Proverbs. Oh, I did help pick berries to sell, but they're almost gone for the year. I want to be a help to Roy and Helen and especially to Carl and Olga. I'm so proud of them—the way they laugh and have such a good time even when they don't know where that next sack of flour is coming from. Never hear them complain. I know You're going to bless them for that. I think You enjoy watching them clear that land and take good care of their little farm just like I do. They're being faithful with what they have, just like you taught, Jesus. I want to be faithful with what you've given me, too. Show me what I can do to be a blessing to my family and neighbors. Please show me how.*

The next morning discouraging thoughts dragged her spirits down like a sinker on a fishing line. How foolish to think that she, a quickly-aging woman, could be an asset to her family. She'd be more and more dependent, not more helpful. *Well,* she sighed, *at least I can take care of myself and Jeanie—and Hank, when he's home.* That was something.

She was picking over raspberries she and Jeanie had picked in Zielkie's woods when Carl suddenly appeared in the doorway. He wanted to know if it would be all right if he built a few shelves in the cellar for Olga's canned goods.

Emma said she didn't see any reason why he couldn't. There was certainly plenty of room, and she told him to take home some canning jars, too. She wouldn't need them all.

As he talked about tomatoes and string beans, Emma stared at his ragged overalls. They had been patched and repatched, but still there were new holes. Carl had never been one to be careful. If his pants caught on barbed wire, he was more likely to keep going than to back up and unhook them.

Wonder if Olga has denim for patches? she thought after Carl had left. She'd hunt in her rag box and see what she could find. Better yet, she'd offer to come over and do some patching. That was something she could do—and darn socks, too! She'd been helping the other girls for years and never thought of it being of much value, but now she saw that preserving was as good as earning. She rummaged in the rag box and smiled. *After all,* she reminded herself, *a penny saved is a penny earned.*

One morning, early in December, after Roy had counted out Emma's third of the cream check and laid it on her table, Emma sat down at Helen's kitchen table. "I just don't know what to do. You know how much it means to Jeanie to have a new dress for Christmas. She's been looking at material for weeks—has a green tweed picked out. But she needs stockings and underwear and there just isn't enough money . . ."

Helen poured coffee and sat down. "We'll think of something. Maybe we can make something over."

Emma took a sip of coffee and shook her head. "I thought of that but I've looked. I don't have a thing to make over."

"I think I have something."

Helen went upstairs and came down with a bright green wool flannel dress. "I haven't worn this for years. It may have a couple of moth holes—"

That afternoon Helen ripped and Emma sponged and pressed the pieces. They agreed to wait until a catalog order came, and they'd put it in one of the bags.

Emma folded the pieces with the largest ones to the outside. "I can cut it when she's in school. She'll never know it wasn't new!"

When the order came, Emma put the material in a bag and piled it with the other items.

"Oh, goody! The order came!" Jeanie squealed when she ran in after school. "Oh! My material!" She pulled it partway out of the bag while Emma held her breath. "It's 'sposed to have little colored spots!"

"They must have had to substitute," she hedged.

Before Emma could stop her, she had pulled the material out of the bag and had begun to unfold it. Of course the whole thing fell apart.

"It's all in pieces!" she wailed.

Carefully, Emma took the bundle from Jeanie's hands and helped her pick up the pieces. "Come here," she said, patting the edge of the bed. "I know you're disappointed. We thought we could fool you. There just isn't enough money for new material."

"But where did it come from?"

"It's a dress of Helen's. We ripped it apart."

"Helen gave *me* her dress?"

171

Emma nodded.

Jeanie grabbed the material, hugged it to her, and ran to find Helen.

She came back a few minutes later, eyes shining. "Oh, Mama! Wasn't that nice of her! It's gonna be so pretty!"

The next morning after Jeanie had gone to school, Emma told Helen, "She was so pleased that you gave her your dress!"

Helen laughed. "Isn't that something! We thought we'd fool her, but she turned around and fooled us!"

Emma went back to her rooms smiling, but for another reason. As Helen had stood sideways in the pantry doorway, Emma saw there'd be another baby in the spring.

CHAPTER 20

THERE WOULD BE *three* new grandchildren come spring, Emma learned when George visited one day in January and told her that Sadie was expecting.

And soon afterward Ed wrote that his and Peggy's special first-anniversary gift would be a baby.

"Lord," Emma whispered as she lay down for a nap, "I know children are a blessing, but neither George nor Sadie is well, and Ed and Peggy have had so little time to get settled—but You know best. Just make these new little ones a blessing."

Ed and Peggy's baby girl Ruth was born on April third; George and Sadie's new daughter on the ninth. They named her Gardia.

Three days later Roy poked his head in Emma's doorway and told her that both the doctor and Helen's mother were on the way. Before noon little Marilyn had arrived.

Emma declared Marilyn to be an especially pretty baby, but Hank mumbled that newborns all looked alike to him.

One evening, as Emma knitted and Hank read the paper, Jeanie said, "How do mothers know they're going to have a baby?"

Emma gulped. "Ah, well—the doctor tells them."

"Oh. But when they get fat, they know. That's why Helen was so fat. The baby was in her tummy."

Hank put down the paper. "It was? Why I thought the doctor brought her in his little black bag!" he said, as Emma shook her fist at him over Jeanie's head.

He hid his taunting grin behind the paper.

When no more questions came, Emma let her breath out slowly. *Oh, dear! Something I haven't thought about.* Her children had simply learned from each other. She couldn't remember teaching them the facts of life.

In June Ed wrote and invited Emma and Jeanie for a week's visit. Carl and Olga offered to take them.

"That's got to be it," Olga said as they hunted for Ed and Peggy's house. "There're kids all over the place!"

Peggy's round face and wide smile had a charm all their own and Emma didn't even think to compare her with Connie.

Olga and Emma were soon working beside Peggy, who rarely left the kitchen, and Emma told her she felt like they had known each other for years instead of hours. Ed beamed.

Jeanie adored baby Ruthie, but Emma heard her tell Shirley that Marilyn was even cuter.

As the women visited, Olga revealed something Emma had already suspected—that *she* would have a new baby in December.

"Jeanie will be so thrilled about Olga's baby," Emma told Peggy the next day. "She idolizes Olga." Emma giggled. "Whenever I want to get her to do something—or not

174

do something—I just tell Olga and she talks her into or out of it.''

Peggy cut up the last potato and rested her hands on the edge of the huge kettle. "Grandma, is it a lot different rearing Jeanie than it was your other children?"

"Oh, I should say it is," Emma said. "Sometimes I think it's been harder than all the other thirteen put together. Seems like Jeanie is always wanting something we can't afford or wanting to do something I don't know anything about. When my children were small, they just went along with the older ones. I didn't have to make all those decisions."

"But isn't there a different sense of responsibility, too?"

"Yes, that, too. I've said it's sort of like having someone look over your shoulder while you work."

Peggy sighed. "That's the way I feel about Ed's children. Every time I have to decide something, I wonder what Connie would have done. Do you think I'll always feel like that?"

"Oh, I don't think so. After all, you've only had them a little over a year, you know. I used to be concerned with what Jeanie's dad would think but, then when he paid so little attention to her, I didn't let it bother me anymore. Still, there is, like you say, a heavier sense of responsibility. Another thing you must remember is that love grows. Don't feel guilty if you don't feel love yet for Ed's children like your own. Get to know them and you'll love them!"

Peggy's face flushed. "I needed to hear that. Sometimes I feel so guilty!"

"Don't you worry! You will have to find a way to spend time with each one alone, though."

"I know. I'm trying. It isn't easy. But, Grandma, Ed is such a good husband and father." She put the potatoes on to boil. "The only time I've really been angry with him was last fall when he took the older children to the fair and spent almost as much as we'd spend for a week's groceries."

They were both laughing when Ed came in. "Aren't you two talked out yet?"

Peggy smiled up at him. "Oh goodness no! I think they should stay another week."

"How about it, Ma?"

Emma shook her head. "I'd like to. I'm having such a nice time and I know Jeanie is, too, but I can't expect Helen to water my garden and, if we don't get rain, I'll lose the few vegetables I've been pampering. But we've got four more days before we have to go home."

As she did at home, Emma took a nap each day after dinner. Usually she didn't sleep, but she welcomed the time to think over the day's happenings and to pray.

Emma was glad she hadn't spent any time being concerned about Ed's choice of a wife. Why, so far, they hadn't discovered anything they didn't agree on. They even worked much the same—completing one task, if at all possible, before beginning another. And, most important, Peggy loved the Lord. And today Emma had discovered that Peggy didn't lack humor.

Ordinarily, Emma would have enjoyed the ride home, but watching nothing but brown, bone-dry grass made her heart ache.

"At least we'll have potatoes," she told Ed. "Roy has worked so hard irrigating the potato field. Doesn't that sound odd—irrigating in our part of the country? You remember the field across the river?"

Ed nodded.

"Well, I don't know if Roy was planning for another dry year when he planted potatoes there this spring or not, but it sure has worked out well. He borrowed a hydraulic ram

176

from Oscar Norlin and built a little dam and ran pipes over into the field. Water runs day and night! Roy keeps changing the hose and the whole field gets watered. Isn't that something?''

But Emma was near tears when she saw her garden. In spite of Helen's efforts, the tomato plants were curled and dry and there were only a few little misshapen green tomatoes on the vines. The beans were completely brown and the cucumber leaves looked as though boiling water had been poured on them. She consoled herself by thinking, *At least we'll have potatoes!*

If Jeanie had been aware of Olga's expected baby, she hadn't said anything to Emma. But when she came home from school December nineteenth and Emma told her Carl and Olga had a little Albert, she didn't act as surprised as Emma thought she'd be. But she certainly was delighted and asked to see him right away.

"Tomorrow," Emma said. She didn't tell her it had been a long hard labor for Olga and that she was exhausted.

My goodness! Carl, a father, Emma mused as she got ready for bed that night. He had been only twelve when Papa died, and now, he was a fine young man.

The yearning to talk to Papa—to tell him all about her problem with Hank, their hard times, the new babies—so much more—welled up in her. "Jesus! Please tell him for me.''

CHAPTER 21

"I THINK THOSE CHICKENS are laying all those eggs because they know how much you need them," Emma said with a twinkle in her eye. Olga had brought in seven eggs one February afternoon when Emma spent the day with her, patching and darning.

Olga hung her wool plaid jacket on a hook by the door and wrote "7" on the February 21 square. "Only two days this month so far that they haven't each laid an egg."

Six of the eleven chicks George and Sadie had given them had been pullets. One little rooster had met an untimely end under the cow's foot. Three others had provided Sunday dinners, and one still strutted and crowed in the little log barn.

"Bet you thought I wasn't ever coming in," Olga said. "When the baby's alone in the house I hurry to get back, but today I did things I've been putting off for weeks."

"Oh, I remember that feeling so well—working with my heart in my throat when the little ones were alone in the house. Those years Papa worked in camp, I had to feed the stock and I just couldn't take the little ones out with me in storms and cold. For a long while I was so scared but I had to learn to trust God to take care of them. I couldn't do it alone.'' Emma held the needle up to the light, threaded it, and continued. "I didn't know it at the time, but this was my lesson in learning to trust. Wasn't long before Al was big enough to be out on his own—coulda fallen in the river, or out of a tree, or got trampled by a horse—'' She waved her hand. "And that was only the beginning. One after the other they grew up and started driving cars and traipsing all over the country—''

Little Albert started to cry and Olga picked him up and held him close. "In other words, *we* can't keep them safe. We have to trust God to take care of them.''

Emma smiled and nodded. "Never did learn that lesson good as I should—have to always drag my thoughts back by the nape of the neck when something new comes up.''

Olga laughed. "And that's pretty often with Jeanie, huh?''

"Oh, yes! Never know what's next. Don't know if it's keeping me young or sending me to my grave a little quicker.''

Olga patted Emma's shoulder. "It's keeping you young! Believe me!''

In April Myrtle had to have an appendectomy. Ella stayed with her in the Marshfield hospital for several days. When Ella got home, she called Emma. "Ma, Jeanie's dad is in the hospital. He's dying, Ma. And he wants to see Jeanie. He looks real bad.''

"Poor man! But I can't let Jeanie see him like that. She gets upset so easily—''

"I tried to tell him that. He just cried.''

179

He was still alive when Myrtle came home, but May seventh the call came. Ed was dead.

Ella and Gertie rode to the funeral with Roy, Emma, and Jeanie. They went to Ed's house before the funeral where the body lay in the living room. His little boy and girl, Jeanie's half-brother and sister, were too young to realize what had happened and played happily outside.

Ed's wife, Amanda, was cordial to them all and there was enough time for Emma to talk quietly with her. Amanda said that, much as she'd miss him, he had suffered so terribly she wouldn't wish him back.

Emma hesitated to talk about Emmie's furniture, but decided it was her only opportunity. When she asked if Jeanie could have it, Amanda said they could come and get it anytime.

Jeanie stood at the casket, teary-eyed but not grief-stricken. She had hardly known her father.

In church Emma remembered it was May 10—exactly ten years since Emmie's death. *Had Emmie lived,* Emma realized, *she would be sitting there in black—a widow at twenty-nine—with, perhaps, several children.* Emmie, not Amanda, would have suffered through Ed's illness these past months.

Jeanie was quiet on the way home, but she didn't appear disturbed. That night, however, after Emma was in bed, she felt a little hand on her shoulder. "Mama . . . I keep seein' him layin' there."

"You can sleep with me tonight."

She crawled over Emma, cuddled close, and slept.

Several weeks later Len got a trailer and hauled Emmie's furniture down from Phillips.

When Emmie's furniture was set up in Jeanie's room, she dragged everyone who set foot in the house up to see the bed with the curved footboard and the vanity dresser with hinged mirrors—and the cedar chest.

Jeanie floated high on her cloud of elation while Emma battled engulfing waves of grief. Seeing the furniture had brought tears to Emma's eyes, but she found she wasn't prepared for the overwhelming pain that swept over her when they went through the cedar chest. Ed had saved all the linens with Emmie's handwork on them—and several of her dresses.

Jeanie listened and questioned as long as Emma was willing to talk about Emmie. When they were nearly through, Jeanie opened a small candy box and shook it. "It's not candy," she said, as Emma laughed and replied that it better not be—after ten years.

Carefully she opened the little box and picked up a tiny piece of crocheted handwork.

"What is it, Mama?" asked Jeanie.

Emma tried to smile. "It's a baby cap . . . She was making it for you."

Tenderly Jeanie laid it back in the box and then threw herself into Emma's lap, sobbing. "I wish I coulda known her!"

Emma patted her head and stroked the soft curls. "You will, *Liebchen*, you will."

That summer, instead of glowering at gloomy skies, Emma gloried in them. Rain was still welcome even though the lawn was greener than usual for July. More important, the pasture and hay fields were green and one could almost hear the corn growing. *Does God ever tire of hearing me say, "Thank-you"?* she wondered.

One August day, with a twinge of jealousy, Emma watched Jeanie trudge up the hill on her way to spend the day at Olga's. Jeanie was often discontented at home—

always wanting to do something that required more of Emma's patience than she could spare.

Emma shook her head and began to clear the table. *How did Olga put up with her?* Only recently Jeanie had dropped all the freshly washed diapers in the dirt on the way to the washline, and it meant using precious water to rinse them all over again. And water had to be carried from the spring a quarter of a mile away, using a wooden yoke across the shoulders with a pail hung at each end, or hauled home in a milk can in Carl's little blue Whippet.

But Emma could understand why Jeanie was drawn to Olga. She knew how to make everyday activities special— something to look forward to. She'd say, "After dinner we'll put a blanket out in the shade and shell peas," or "When little Albert wakes up, we'll take a walk in the woods."

That evening when Jeanie came home with Carl, she raced in yelling, "Mama? Do you have an extra needle? Olga was helping me sew a doll dress and I was threading the needle and it fell right down the crack in the floor." She made a dramatic gesture and sighed. "It was her *last* needle!"

Emma rummaged in her sewing cabinet and found a pack of needles. She stuck three of them in a piece of cloth and was about to hand it to Jeanie when Carl came. He stuck them in his shirt pocket and grinned. "Thanks, Ma. Dreamed the other night that the cracks in that floor were so wide I had to jump from one board to another."

Emma laughed. "Oh, dear! If you had to jump, imagine what little Olga would have had to do!"

"Thought that lumber was dry, but it just keeps shrinking."

"Would be nice if you could get linoleum for that kitchen end."

"Well, if enough people die—" he said with a twinkle in his eye.

"Oh, you! How you talk!" she chided as he grinned at her over his shoulder on his way out the door.

Carl's grave-digging job had certainly been a blessing.

Olga had said, "We start wondering where the next sack of flour is coming from and then somebody dies and Carl gets three dollars for digging the grave. Oh, I don't mean I'm glad when someone dies—but I can't help being grateful for the money."

The last week in August Emma told Ella, "I'll walk over one day this week. I know how much work you have before your anniversary party. At least I can help you with some mending and it will be the last time the girls can be together before school starts."

Ella said she'd be glad to have them come. They could plan to stay for supper and Henry would drive them home.

"What on earth do you kids find to do in that woods all the time?" Emma asked Jeanie as they walked up the last hill toward Ella's.

"Lotsa things. We swing on saplings and we explore 'n build houses and play hide-and-seek. Can I run ahead?"

"Oh, go on." *Ah, yes. Let her run. Need to be alone a few minutes.*

Emma smiled as she watched Jeanie's little legs fly along. Such energy! The hill seemed unusually steep today. She stopped, only vaguely aware of her pulse pounding in her ears, and smiled up at the neat white house and big red barn and thought of those nine busy lives. So much to be thankful for—hay in the mow, silage in the silo, oats in the bin, and plenty of potatoes.

"Lord, I'm thankful," she talked right out loud. God seemed especially close today. "I can walk these two miles—don't even have to ask anyone to drive me. I can do

183

my own housework and take care of Jeanie and even help with milking and go and mend for the girls. And that special peace You give me! You're all I need! O Jesus, Jesus," she whispered—eyes closed now. "You are *here*—in me, around me. I can't explain it. I would come to You anytime. Don't even think of it as dying—just walking into Your world, like walking through a doorway right to You. O, Lord, to think of living like this—with this perfect peace *all the time!*

"But, Lord," her voice choked on a sob. "I want all my children to know You like this. I want it so bad—and it hurts so much when they won't listen—when they think if they give their whole lives to You that You'll take all the fun out of it. They don't know! They just don't know that their idea of fun is nothing compared to the joy You give. O Lord, why did you let *me* know You like this?"

What was that? She thought she heard Jeanie.

She looked up and saw Jeanie waving to her from the driveway but she couldn't hear what she was calling to her. "I'm coming," she called, and began walking.

She blew her nose and dried her tears. Ella wouldn't understand—not yet.

She looked up at the woolly clouds. "Father, if I long to have them know You and love You and trust You, how much more You must long for that! I trust You!"

Excitement bubbled up in her as she walked and thought about the anniversary party. She could see Henry and Ella and the seven children lining up for pictures. Twenty-five years—seemed like yesterday when Ella was a young girl working beside her. "Whatever would I have done without her," she said to herself and began to sing softly as she walked. "Shall we gather at the riv . . . er. That beautiful, that beautiful riv . . . er. Gather with the saints at the riv . . . er that flows by the throne of God . . ."

CHAPTER 22

THE DAY OF THE ANNIVERSARY PARTY Emma thanked God for a clear day, even though she had spent a restless night. She tried to think of what she had eaten the day before that might have upset her, but couldn't recall anything unusual. She drank tea instead of barley coffee that morning, nibbled a little toast, and decided that physical discomfort would not rob her of this exciting day anymore than she would have allowed it to rob her twenty-five years ago when the house teemed with wedding guests. Oh, if Papa could only see Ella now—a fine woman, a beloved mother.

I'll be careful what I eat, Emma reminded herself as they drove in the driveway and up the hill, already lined with cars.

So many dear ones she saw all too seldom—Len, Nora and the children; John, Esther, and little Jean; Clara and Walter; and so many more. She forgot all about not feeling well as she greeted them.

Later, although the food looked delicious, Emma decided

to wait until others were served before she ate. She found a quiet corner in the living room—nearly everyone was outside—and tried to ignore the tight feeling and twinges of pain across her chest. Surely she wasn't getting pleurisy again. She'd never had it in warm weather. *Oh, well, no sense sitting here thinking about it. I'll go eat a little something.*

She laughed and talked with her niece Leah while they were in line. When she noticed the forks were almost gone, she slipped out of the line, picked up a dishtowel, and began drying some.

Jeanie dashed in, laughing so hard she could hardly talk. "Oh, Mama! You shoulda heard—"

Emma didn't hear anymore. An invisible vise had clamped her chest in a crushing pain.

"Go . . . play . . ." she gasped and staggered toward Ella's bedroom. The bed . . . the bed . . . if only she could make it to the bed. She heard Jeanie scream and arms and voices were everywhere, surrounding her, lifting her.

"Don't lay her down. You could kill her!"

"Someone! Get more pillows!"

"Call the doctor!"

"You'll be all right, Emma . . ."

"Don't struggle, Ma," Roy urged.

She caught a glimpse of Jeanie's wide-eyed horror. She couldn't talk but her mind was pleading, pleading, *O, Lord! Not yet! Not yet! She needs me!*

The pain—her arm, shoulder, even her jaw. And the terrible crushing weight on her chest. Someone spoke the words she had already thought: "Heart attack."

Faces—voices—"Breathe deep! Relax!" Would it ever end? If it weren't for Jeanie, she'd so gladly let go.

"Can't reach Dr. McKinnon," she heard.

Someone wiped her tears.

"Dr. Baker from Rib Lake is coming."

Jeanie? Where was Jeanie? Was she all right? She tried to ask, but she couldn't get the words out.

Pain—pain—hard to breathe. So many people! *Lord, help me!*

"The doctor's here."

Hands opening her dress, gentle hands moving a stethoscope over her chest . . .

A sting in her arm. The vise releasing, releasing—drifting, drifting—

Dark. Quiet.

"Ella?"

"I'm here, Ma."

"I'm so sorry."

"Don't you worry. You're more important than any old party. Here, drink a little of this."

"So tired—"

"Ella?"

"No, Emma. It's Clara. Just rest."

"What time is it?"

"Almost five."

"Supper time?"

"No. Five in the morning."

"Oh, dear, you should be home in bed!"

"Take a little drink of water."

Emma turned her head away. Hadn't better drink. Would have to use the bedpan. Afraid to move.

"Pain, Emma?"

She nodded and struggled to speak. "My little girl— what will she do? I'm all she has."

Clara squeezed Emma's hand. "No, Emma. Who does she really belong to?"

Tired—so tired. Pain. Clara's words slipping past her— Daylight. Footsteps. Doors closing.

"Mama?" Jeanie beside the bed. Ella coaxing her out. *Poor baby! What will she do?*

Faces at the doorway—Roy, Helen—Carl, Olga—Hank, chin quivering—Al, Mamie, all so quiet, patting her hand, leaving quickly.

I must be dying. My little girl! What will happen? Clara. What did Clara say? Have to remember . . .

Night again. Lamp casting gnome-like shadows on the wall.

Ella's soft hand smoothing her brow. Poor Ella. Must be so tired.

Daylight.

Jeanie's stricken little face. *Must try to smile—tell her to go to school. Pain!*

Quiet. Alone. *Lord, I don't understand. I'm all she has!* No, Clara had asked, "Who does she *really* belong to?"

I see. I understand! She belongs to You, Lord! You will take care of her. You will take care of her!

So tired. Hard to breathe. Want to sleep and sleep. *Jesus, I'd like to come to You—be with You all the time—feel that wonderful feeling I felt up in the woods.*

"Ma, try to drink a little tea."

She turned her head away again.

Roy's voice now. "Ma, you drink this! We can't do it for you!" She took a few sips.

Night. The shadows again. The smell of the kerosene lamp.

Drifting—drifting—walking in a flower-strewn meadow. Beautiful! Papa's strong arm around her. Happy! So much to tell him! *There must have been a million times I wanted to tell you something, but you weren't there!*

Emmie—running toward them!

"Ma! Please take a drink."

Tears. "Want to talk to Emmie!"

Ella's voice shook. "Did you forget? Emmie's gone!"

"I know. I mean when I get there."

Daylight. Jeanie holding her hand in both of hers. "Mama? You better?"

Smile. Nod.

"Ma, we've been trying to get Dr. McKinnon. Talked to him on the phone. He says to lie still—but you must drink. He'll come soon as he can."

Ella, always fussing. Pulling sheets. Washing her. Trying to get her to drink.

"Leave me alone!"

"I'm sorry, Ma. I have to."

"What day is it?"

"Tuesday."

"Ella, I want to tell you something. I'm not afraid to die."

"I know."

Quiet. Alone. Jeanie's terrified little face. *Father, take care of her*. Tears running down. Too tired to wipe them.

That odor—disinfectant. The doctor!

"Well, let's see what goes on here!" His voice bounced off the walls of the little room. "Sit up a bit now. Breathe through your open mouth. Again. Again. Pain?"

"Uh-huh."

"Hard to breathe?"

"Uh-huh."

"It will take awhile, but you'll be all right."

Emma's eyes flew open. "I'm not going to die?"

His laugh boomed. "Not now, you aren't!" He patted her hand. "A blood clot shut off the circulation to part of your heart, but it will heal. Other blood vessels will take over, in time."

"They will? What should I do?"

"I'll tell your daughter. You mind her. Got to get you

back on your feet." He smiled at Jeanie, hovering by the doorway. "You've got an important job to do!"

Alone again. *I'm not going to die. Little by little I'll move. I'll walk. Oh, but I don't feel like struggling! I wanted to be with Papa—to talk with Emmie.*

Night again. Pain still there.

"Ma. Here's some farina. Will you eat a little?

Too tired. Want to sleep. Dream of Papa—Emmie.

"Mama? Aunt Ella's cryin' 'cause you won't eat."

"Tell her I'll try."

Someone always trying to get her to drink—eat.

Night again. Restless. Right leg cramping.

"Ma! What is it?"

"Leg cramp."

"Swing your legs out! Here! Sit up!"

"Ah, it's going away. I'm sorry."

"You just call! Don't try to sit up alone."

Twice more cramps awakened her. She must have groaned because Ella came. Poor Ella.

Morning.

"Grandma?" Myrtle leaned over her. "Mama wants to know if you'll eat a little oatmeal."

"I'll try."

Myrtle turned to go. "Myrtle! You help your Mama real good now!"

"I will, Grandma!"

Days blur together. So many faces. So many questions. "How are you? Still have pain? You want some water?"

Clara was there at night again when her legs cramped.

"Clara, I know now what you meant. She's not really mine. Our Lord will take care of her 'cause she belongs to Him."

"Emma, listen to me. You are not going to die! You will get stronger and stronger."

"Too tired—"

Morning.

"Ma, Clara's going to stay right by you while you sit in the chair and I change the bed."

"Glad to sit up. My back aches."

"Take it slow! There now. Dizzy?"

"A little."

Good to be back in bed again.

Jeanie—sobbing quietly beside the bed.

"There, there, *Liebchen.* I'm going to get well. The doctor said so."

Little arms hugging her. "Oh, Mama!"

Evening again. "Ma. I'm going to help you sit up in the chair again. Maybe your legs won't cramp tonight."

Her left leg cramped once but she didn't groan—just swung her legs out and sat up by herself. She smiled when she lay back down. Big accomplishment!

The next day she sat up three times and walked a few steps—feet feeling full of pins and needles. Her heart flipped some but there was only slight pain.

Each day a little more. Out to the living room. The next day to the kitchen rocker. So weak—but better. Much better.

Days were long now. Things had been going so well! How could life change so fast?

Tired of lying down. If only she could move that little piece of wallpaper over the door—just a bit so it would match the next one. She moved it, mentally, a thousand times. Got to look at seams that do match. I shouldn't always look for what's wrong with things.

Got to try to walk alone. Have to walk alone before I can go home.

"Ma! What are you doing?" Ella shouted, dropping a plate in the dishpan.

"Got to start walking on my own," she said, sitting down heavily in the kitchen rocker. "You know . . . I feel like I've come out of a long dark tunnel." She sighed. "It's good to be back in the light. I hadn't even noticed the beautiful autumn leaves until today."

It was pleasant, those days, to sit in Ella's living room and look out at the countless shades of gold, crimson, and the lingering spots of green. She welcomed the opportunity to ponder, plan, and pray.

Lord, something has happened to me. I don't feel that fear that I'll die before Jeanie grows up even though it seems like I was so close to dying. You took it away! I trust You to take care of her. And I trust you to help me get this body back in shape, too. I know it won't be easy, but I can't be a blessing to anyone layin' around here—and You know how much I want to help where I can. I want to take care of Jeanie and help with milking and feed chickens and even go berrypicking again. One more thing—if I start feeling sorry for myself, shake me up good!

"I feel so strong," she told Ella as the sipped tea that afternoon, "that I think I could go home and clean my whole house."

Ella chuckled. "I'm afraid you'd change your mind in a hurry once you got started. You know it's going to take time to get your strength back."

Emma was in bed when Jeanie got home.

"Mama? You sleepin'?"

"No. I'm thinking. I think it's time for us to go home—if you're willing to help me carry wood and water.

Jeanie squeezed Emma's hand. "Oh, I'll help! I'll help!"

Emma smiled . . . and nodded. "Go get Aunt Ella."

ABOUT THE AUTHOR

JEANETTE GILGE, author, writing instructor, and lecturer, began studying writing when her youngest of six children was eight years of age. Now, seventeen years later, she has published four books and numerous articles and stories. A widow, Jeanette lives in the family home in Maywood, Illinois.

Like *The Waltons* and the *Little House* stories, the people in this book really lived. The locale, which is listed under Wisconsin historical sites as Meier's Yesterday House, is visited by hundreds each year. *Call Her Blessed* was born out of love for the grandmother who reared her. Little Jeanie is Jeanette!

A Letter To Our Readers

Dear Reader:

Pioneering is an exhilarating experience, filled with opportunities for exploring new frontiers. The Zondervan Corporation is proud to be the first major publisher to launch a series of inspirational romances designed to inspire and uplift as well as to provide wholesome entertainment. In order that we might better contribute to your reading enjoyment, we would appreciate your taking a few minutes to respond to the following questions and return to:

> Anne Severance, Editor
> Serenade/Saga Books
> 749 Templeton Drive
> Nashville, Tennessee   37205

1. Did you enjoy reading CALL HER BLESSED?
   ☐ Very much. I would like to see more books by this author!
   ☐ Moderately
   ☐ I would have enjoyed it more if _____

2. Where did you purchase this book? _____

3. What influenced your decision to purchase this book?

   ☐ Cover   ☐ Back cover copy
   ☐ Title   ☐ Friends
   ☐ Publicity   ☐ Other _____

4. Please rate the following elements (from 1 to 10):

- ☐ Heroine
- ☐ Hero
- ☐ Setting
- ☐ Plot
- ☐ Inspirational theme
- ☐ Secondary characters

5. Which settings do you prefer?

_____   _____

_____   _____

6. What are some inspirational themes you would like to see treated in future Serenade books?

_____   _____

_____   _____

7. Would you be interested in reading other Serenade/Serenata or Serenade/Saga Books?

- ☐ Very interested
- ☐ Moderately interested
- ☐ Not interested

8. Please indicate your age range:

- ☐ Under 18
- ☐ 18–24
- ☐ 25–34
- ☐ 35–45
- ☐ 46–55
- ☐ Over 55

9. Would you be interested in a Serenade book club? If so, please give us your name and address:

Name _____

Occupation _____

Address _____

City _____ State _____ Zip _____